Kim knocked softly, then stepped into the doorway.

Brandon was pacing. A pair of well-worn jeans hung low on his lean hips, his broad chest shirtless, muscles bunching in his arms as he clenched the phone.

He pivoted as if he sensed she was there, then his gaze locked with hers. His eyes glittered with turmoil and other emotions she couldn't define. But his hard, lean, muscular body robbed her breath and vaulted her back to a time when she would have run into his arms without a second's hesitation.

So much had changed.

RITA HERRON

COWBOY IN THE EXTREME

TORONTO NEW YORK LONDON
AMSTERDAM PARIS SYDNEY HAMBURG
STOCKHOLM ATHENS TOKYO MILAN MADRID
PRAGUE WARSAW BUDAPEST AUCKLAND

To my cousin Linda for being a great cousin,
teacher and reader!

Recycling programs
for this product may
not exist in your area.

ISBN-13: 978-0-373-69596-6

COWBOY IN THE EXTREME

ABOUT THE AUTHOR

Award-winning author Rita Herron wrote her first book when she was twelve, but didn't think real people grew up to be writers. Now she writes so she doesn't have to get a *real* job. A former kindergarten teacher and workshop leader, she traded her storytelling to kids for writing romance, and now she writes romantic comedies and romantic suspense. She lives in Georgia with her own romance hero and three kids. She loves to hear from readers, so please write her at P.O. Box 921225, Norcross, GA 30092-1225, or visit her website, www.ritaherron.com.

Books by Rita Herron

HARLEQUIN INTRIGUE

†Nighthawk Island
‡‡Guardian Angel Investigations
%Guardian Angel Investigations: Lost and Found
**Bucking Bronc Lodge

CAST OF CHARACTERS

Brandon Woodstock—This rough-and-tumble cowboy had his reasons for leaving Kim five years ago. But now she and their daughter—a baby he never knew about—are in danger. He will give his life to protect them; but will he ever earn Kim's trust and love again?

Kim Long—She needs Brandon to help her find her daughter, but she cannot lose her heart to him again.

Lucy Long—All this four-year-old wants is to come home to her mommy and daddy.

Carter Flagstone—Prison escapee, Brandon's former best friend and Kim's former lover. Has he come back to claim the little girl he believes is his and get revenge against Brandon for not giving him an alibi and keeping him out of jail?

Marty Canterberry Woodstock—Rumors claim Brandon's ex is on the verge of marrying again. Are the rumors true, or is she still in love with Brandon?

Herbert Baxter—He owned the land where the kidnapper demanded Kim make the ransom drop. Is he behind the kidnapping?

Farley Wills—Brandon's ranch hand recently came into a large sum of money. Was it a payment for the kidnapping?

Boyd Tombs—He hasn't shown up for work since the kidnapping. Did he abduct the little girl for the money?

Chapter One

"Carter escaped from prison."

"What?" Brandon Woodstock's heart began to race as he heard the worry in his best friend's voice. "How?"

"I don't have all the details yet," Johnny said, clearly agitated. "After the rodeo, I went to see him in prison and gave him the number of a P.I. I hired to investigate his case."

"And he accepted your help?" Brandon asked. "I thought he hated both of us." Brandon sank into the desk chair at the Bucking Bronc Lodge's office wishing he was home on his own spread. He would be in a few hours. He couldn't handle being on the ranch when Johnny's sister, Kim, was here.

Kim, his first love, his *only* love.

The woman who'd betrayed him with Carter. The woman who'd had Carter's child instead of his.

That hurt the worst....

"Not at first," Johnny said. "But I convinced him to take the P.I.'s card and talk to him."

"Now you believe he was innocent of murder?"

The three of them, Carter, Johnny and him, had been inseparable as kids. Kim had tagged along, the tomboy little sister, and aggravated the hell out of them.

Until she'd hit her teens and become a raging beauty. He'd fallen for her, then slept with her, much to Johnny's consternation, although eventually Johnny had accepted them as a couple.

Then he'd made the worst mistake of his life by leaving her for another woman, one he'd thought would help him climb from the gutter of his trailer-park-trash past to success.

And it had worked initially. But then Brandon realized he'd crawled into bed with a snake and had been running from the venomous bite ever since.

Still, Carter had wasted no time. He'd stepped in to fill his shoes...in Kim's bed.

That affair had ripped apart their friendship.

Soon after, Carter had been arrested and convicted of murder. Carter had begged him and Johnny to lie and give him an alibi. Their refusal to perjure themselves had cemented the end of their friendship with Carter.

Johnny cleared his throat. "After seeing the way Rachel's ex bought off the cops and framed her for trying to kill him, I started thinking that someone could have framed Carter."

"So did the P.I. turn up anything?" Brandon asked, getting back on track.

"No, he didn't have time. Carter met with him once and told him about this woman he claims he was with the night of the murder. Carter recognized her in one of the photos of the rodeo."

The newspaper featuring the rodeo was spread on Brandon's desk. He'd tried to avoid looking at the picture of Kim and her little girl, Lucy. It hurt too damn much.

He steered his mind back to Carter. "This woman was at the Bucking Bronc Lodge?"

"In the stands," Johnny said. "She's Native American. Carter claimed they had a one-night stand, and that he saw her the night of the murder."

"Did Troy find her?"

"I don't know. Troy was working on locating her, but two days after he visited Carter, Troy was found dead."

The air in Brandon's lungs tightened. "He was murdered?"

A tense moment passed; then Johnny mumbled, "Yes."

Brandon chewed the inside of his cheek, contemplating everything that had happened. "Maybe he was onto something that got him killed."

"My thoughts exactly." Johnny's footsteps clattered, and Brandon realized he was pacing.

Anxious himself, Brandon went to the bar in the corner, poured a shot of whiskey and swirled the amber liquid in the glass. He hated to distrust Carter, but before the arrest five years ago, Carter had been drinking too much, constantly skirting trouble. He'd even blacked out a few times and let his rage rule his actions.

The way Carter had attacked him a few times replayed through Brandon's head, and more doubts nagged at him. "Or maybe Troy found out Carter committed the murder, and Carter had someone kill Troy."

Johnny sighed. "Or maybe Carter thinks Troy died because of him and it's time he found out the truth."

"Then he's looking for this woman?"

"Probably," Johnny said. "And he has to be desperate. I raised his hopes and so did Troy. And now Troy's dead. That's enough to do a number on anyone."

"Dammit. We both know how Carter gets when he's

bottled up with anger." The very reason both of them had questioned Carter's innocence five years ago.

"Yeah, I know." Johnny sounded frustrated. "I just wanted to warn you. Two other prisoners escaped and a guard was wounded. His weapon was stolen."

Brandon cursed. "So Carter may be armed, and the cops probably have orders to shoot to kill."

"That about sizes it up," Johnny hissed. "Carter has to be scared. Whether he went willingly or not, he's on the run, he's pissed, he needs help, and he—"

"May show up here." Brandon downed the liquor. Hell, Carter would probably blame him for this trouble, too. He removed his gun from the desk drawer where he'd locked it and stuffed it in the back of his jeans.

If Carter came looking for a fight, Brandon would be ready.

KIM LONG TRIED TO IGNORE the rapid tapping of her heart as her four-year-old daughter, Lucy, taped the photos of the rodeo onto her bedroom wall. Ever since the rodeo, Lucy had been asking questions about her Uncle Johnny's friend Brandon.

"I wants to learn to do twicks like him," Lucy chimed. "He was co-ol."

Lucy had picked up that word from Kenny, Johnny's fiancée's six-year-old son who Lucy trailed after like a puppy.

Just as Kim had trailed after Johnny and Brandon and Carter when they'd been kids. The boys had dubbed themselves the Three Musketeers, and Kim had begged to be the fourth. They had refused, although they had tolerated her, mostly because she'd been such a tomboy.

Then they'd all grown up and everything had gone awry.

Lucy twirled a pigtail around one finger. "Mommy, will Uncle Johnny's friend teach me?"

Oh, God…she didn't think so. "I doubt it, baby. He has his own ranch to run. But maybe Uncle Johnny will."

Lucy poked her lips into a pout. "But he gots his own family now. He gots Kenny and if they gets another baby he won't ever see us."

Kim tipped her daughter's chin up with her thumb, her heart aching. She'd known that one day Johnny would have his own family and was thrilled for him. No one deserved to find happiness and love more than her older brother. That was one reason she'd taken the job at the Bucking Bronc. She and Lucy couldn't live with Johnny forever. And he would never ask them to leave. He was too protective.

She just hadn't realized how much Lucy would miss him.

How much Lucy had missed not having a real daddy of her own.

"Your Uncle J will always have time for us, sugar." She kept the tears at bay. "And we'll visit him and Rachel and Kenny all the time." In fact, every time Brandon volunteered at the Bucking Bronc, they'd make the trek to Johnny's ranch. She couldn't be around Brandon and not ache for the life she'd dreamed they might share one day.

Lucy's eyes grew sleepy. "Pwomise?"

"Promise." Kim hugged her, then tucked Lucy's lamb beside her and covered her with her favorite pink blanket. Lucy snuggled down under the covers, and Kim stroked her dark red hair until she fell asleep.

Exhausted from helping reorganize and clean between camps, she went to her room and crawled in bed. But as she closed her eyes, images of Brandon plagued her.

Brandon at age ten staggering up to the fort they had built, bloody from another beating from his old man. Brandon at thirteen teaching her how to shoot a BB gun. Brandon at sixteen galloping across the pasture and showing off the tricks he'd learned from the rancher who'd given him a job and some self-respect. Brandon entering into some extreme fighting contests hoping to make a buck to get him out of his hellhole.

Then the night of the barbecue. The night Brandon had first kissed her. The night the budding romance and passion kindling between them had become more...

But another memory intruded, one so painful it was like being doused with ice water. The night Brandon had broken her heart.

She closed her eyes and drifted into a fitful sleep. In the nightmare, she was riding in the open pasture, but it was dark and she'd lost her way. She couldn't see which direction to go and someone was chasing her....

Suddenly she startled awake, her heart drumming. Outside, the wind shook the roof and something scraped the windowpane. A tree branch? One of the shutters loose?

Then another sound echoed in the silence...a door squeaking?

She vaulted up in bed, searching the darkness as she scanned the room. The dresser, the chair...the closet door was closed. Everything was just as she'd left it.

A faint sliver of moonlight seeped through the blinds, making the silhouette of the trees outside look gigantic and ominous. Had she imagined the noise? Dreamt it?

No…another sound…soft, muffled like footsteps. The floor squeaked in the living room.

Her pulse pounded, and she jumped up, slowly cracked open her door, and peered through the dimly lit hall. A shadow moved across the den.

Her breath caught as fear shot through her.

Lucy…

She reached for her cell phone, wishing she had a gun. But her shotgun was locked in the gun cabinet in the den.

She tiptoed to the bathroom and grabbed her hair spray, then eased through the door and crept across the hall to Lucy's room. The floor squeaked again, and fear nearly choked her.

They'd had some problems with vagrants and a vandal on the Bucking Bronc property.

Was one of them breaking in now?

She eased the door shut and locked it, determination setting in. He could steal whatever he wanted. But she wouldn't let him hurt her daughter.

Lucy was still sleeping, and Kim lifted her in her arms and carried her into the walk-in closet.

"Mommy?" Her daughter stirred, her face wrinkling with confusion, and Kim rocked her gently.

"Shh, baby, it's okay. We need to be quiet and hide for a minute."

Lucy clutched the lamb, squinting at her through the hazy darkness. Panic tugged at Kim. Her first instinct was to call Johnny, but he'd already left for his place.

Her hands shook as she punched in Brody's office number. Brody was the primary owner of the ranch and could get here faster than a 911 call could send somebody.

A voice answered on the second ring, deep and gruff. "Bucking Bronc Lodge."

Kim froze, hand shaking. Oh, God…it wasn't Brody. That was Brandon's voice.

"Hello?"

The rattling sound grew louder. Whoever was outside was going to break down the door!

Kim pressed her mouth to the phone's mouthpiece, terrified the intruder would hear her. "It's Kim," she whispered. "There's an intruder in my cabin."

Lucy jerked awake, her eyes wide with terror. "Mommy?"

"Shh, baby." Kim tucked Lucy's head against her chest, her heart racing.

Brandon made a shocked sound in his throat. "I'll be right there." The phone clicked to silence, and Kim closed her eyes and said a silent prayer that he would reach them in time.

But a second later, the bedroom door rattled. Then came the sound of the doorknob being turned.

"Mommy!" Lucy's nails dug into Kim's arms, and she braced herself to fight.

A loud noise—a body slamming against the door— made her jerk her head up.

Oh, God, he was going to break down the door…

BRANDON'S THROAT clogged with fear as he jogged outside to his SUV. Dammit, Johnny said they'd had trouble on the ranch the last couple of weeks, but since Rachel's ex-husband had been caught, he'd assumed the trouble was over.

What if someone had broken in and hurt Kim?

Pure terror seized him at the thought, and he stomped on the accelerator and raced toward her cabin, punching in 911 as he went.

A second later a dispatch officer came over the line.

"We have a break-in at the Bucking Bronc Lodge. Get the sheriff over here fast." He stayed on the line long enough to give more specific instructions, then disconnected and swerved onto the road to Kim's.

Dust spewed and gravel flew as he bounced over the ruts, bypassing the stables and dining hall, then screeching to a halt outside Kim's cabin. He looked out the windows, the dark exterior and woods.

He didn't see a car or stranger, only horses galloping across pasture land, but there were acres and acres of places to hide. Was the intruder still inside?

Easing the car door open, he slid out, removed his gun and crept toward the cabin, wielding his weapon in case the culprit jumped out in attack.

Seconds later, horse hooves pounded the dirt behind the cabin.

Dammit, he wanted to chase the bastard, but what if there was more than one?

He had to check on Kim and her daughter first.

He held his breath as he inched open the door. Darkness bathed the interior, and he searched blindly to see if someone was inside. A lamp was overturned, broken. A twig snapped beneath his boots, and the wind whistled through an open window. Was that how the jerk got in?

The sound of a child's soft cries echoed from one of the bedrooms. A terrified sound that made Brandon's blood turn to ice. Lucy.

Was she simply frightened or had the intruder hurt her or Kim?

Chapter Two

Panic bolted through Kim. Whoever had broken in was determined to find her and Lucy.

But the sound of a car engine rumbled outside, then a siren wailed, a door slammed and more footsteps pounded.

Lucy trembled against her, and Kim soothed her. "It's all right, baby."

Brandon's gruff voice echoed through the house. "Kim, it's all right. Where are you?"

Relief surged through her, and she jumped up and hurried to unlock the door. Lucy clung to her, her head trying to bore a hole in Kim's chest.

The doorknob twisted, and he knocked on the wood. "Kim, answer me," Brandon asked. "Are you hurt?"

"I'm okay, just give me a minute." Adjusting Lucy on her hip, she flipped the lock and threw open the door. When she saw Brandon in the doorway looking worried and so damn handsome and big and strong, she was so relieved she almost collapsed into his arms. "Thank you for coming," she said on a ragged breath.

He took a step forward as if to reach for her and the years of hurt and pain fell away. She ached to have him hold her again, to make everything all right, to have him love her.

But his pale green eyes, eyes that reminded her of their past, of the hurt and betrayal between them, skated over her, then down to Lucy and she stiffened.

He'd never met Lucy before. What if he took one look and knew the truth?

Brandon tensed, gripping his hands into fists. "Are you two okay?"

Kim stroked her daughter's back, swaying back and forth rocking her. "Yes. Just frightened."

Brandon gestured toward the living room. "Come on, let's go into the den. Then you can tell me what happened."

Kim's legs felt shaky as she walked to the living room and sank onto the couch. Brandon flipped on the kitchen light, and she blinked to adjust her eyes. The sight of the broken lamp and dirt on the floor made her stomach knot with renewed fear.

"Mommy?" Lucy lifted her head slightly, tears streaking her cheeks, and Kim wiped them away with her hand.

"It's okay, honey. We're safe. You can go back to sleep." Lucy sighed, then seemed to accept her mother's answer and huddled against her chest in a tiny ball.

Blue lights from the sheriff's approaching car swirled outside, streaking the window. The sound of the engine clicking off echoed in the tense silence; then seconds later, the sheriff appeared at the door.

Brandon went to meet him. "Sheriff, I'm Brandon Woodstock, Johnny and Brody's friend. I was at the main house when Kim called about the break-in."

Sheriff McRae introduced himself, then followed Brandon over to the sofa, where she sat trying to compose herself. But having someone try to break into her cabin and seeing Brandon so close that she could touch him had her nerves tied in knots.

"What happened?" Sheriff McRae asked. "Did you see anyone?"

Kim swallowed hard. The sheriff was a big guy with a barrel chest and eyes that cut through her. "No, I was in bed when I heard a noise," Kim said. "I heard footsteps and the lamp crashed to the floor, so I ran to Lucy's room and locked her door. Then we hid in the closet."

Sheriff McRae shifted on the balls of his feet. "Let me take a look around." He examined the lock, then stooped down to study the dirt marring the wood entryway. "It looks like he picked the lock."

"Johnny said there were problems on the ranch before," Brandon said. "A fire and fencing cut."

"Yes, I've been investigating those incidents," Sheriff McRae said. "This could be related. I'll get a crime kit and dust for fingerprints."

He glanced back at the door. "Was the intruder still here when you arrived, Woodstock?"

Brandon shook his head. "I heard a horse galloping away in the back, but I was worried about Kim and her daughter so I checked inside first."

Sheriff McRae nodded, then angled his head toward Kim.

"Ma'am, can you think of anyone who'd want to hurt you? Do you have any enemies?"

Kim shook her head. "No."

"How about a husband or boyfriend?"

Kim felt Brandon's gaze burning through her, and gritted her teeth. "No."

Sheriff McRae raised a brow. "No ex-husband who might want the child?"

She knew he was thinking about Rachel's situation, that her ex had been stalking her and tried to kidnap their son. "I've never been married."

"What about the little girl's father?"

Kim glared at him for asking such a question in front of her daughter. "I said no."

"Wait a minute," Brandon cut in, his tone worried. "Johnny called earlier to warn me, Kim. There was a prison break. Carter escaped."

Kim gasped, perspiration beading on her neck. "I have to talk to Johnny."

The sheriff gave her an odd look, but she didn't wait to explain. She settled Lucy on the sofa and covered her with an afghan, then took her phone and stepped onto the porch.

The sheriff's questions were too probing. Too close to home. She had to do something. Get away. Hide.

If Carter had escaped and knew she was here, he might have come after Lucy.

BRANDON RECOGNIZED the fear and panic in Kim's eyes and wanted to comfort her. But he had given up that right when he'd left her and married Marty.

Besides, she had slept with Carter. Just the thought of her in Carter's arms, in his *bed,* roused his anger.

Hell, if Carter was coming here to see his daughter, Brandon could hardly blame him.

It was exactly what he would do if Lucy had been his child, and he'd been locked up for years, unable to watch her grow up and spend holidays and birthdays with her.

Had Kim carried Lucy to the prison to see Carter? What had she told the little girl about her father?

Pain knifed through him, an ache so raw that he had to suck air through his teeth to stem a moan.

He would never have a child of his own. He couldn't risk it.

Not knowing whether he might pass on the same genetic disorder that had tormented his younger sister. Not after losing her to it…

It was the final straw that had ended his marriage to Marty. She had wanted a family. He had adamantly refused. He could not chance bringing a child into the world only to watch the child suffer the way Joanie had.

Besides, he'd known it was a last frantic attempt on Marty's part to tie him to her.

God knows, he'd wanted to love her.

But he hadn't been able to and she'd known it.

Because he'd given his heart to Kim years ago, and he'd never gotten it back.

"What's going on?" Sheriff McRae asked. "You mean the prison break earlier at the state pen where a guard was shot?"

Brandon nodded. "I'm afraid so."

"Do you know one of the prisoners?"

"Yes. Carter Flagstone." He tightened his fists to control his temper. "He and Johnny Long and Kim and I grew up together."

Sheriff McRae grimaced and folded his arms. "You think he'll come to you for help?"

Brandon made a sarcastic sound. "Hardly. We had a falling-out a few years back. After he was arrested, we lost touch." Because Brandon had hated his guts for sleeping with Kim. And Carter had accused him of not giving him an alibi because of that night. It was a pretty messed-up story.

"This falling out..." Sheriff McRae cocked his head sideways. "It wouldn't happen to be about Kim?"

Brandon heaved a weary sigh. "Yeah, it would. That and the fact that Johnny and I didn't stand up for him in court like he thought we should have."

"So you think he's looking for revenge?"

Brandon hated to bad-mouth his old buddy. But Carter had been trouble in the old days, drinking and fighting, conning his way into women's beds, starting bar brawls, and then having blackouts. No telling how prison life had hardened him. Like Johnny said, he must be desperate.

"It's possible," Brandon said. He glanced at the sleeping little redhead on the sofa all curled up beneath the blanket hugging her stuffed lamb to her. "Either that, or he came here to see his daughter."

KIM PRESSED THE PHONE to her ear in a white-knuckled grip, keeping an eye on Lucy from the doorway of the porch. The sheriff went to his car and returned a moment later, murmuring he was going to check for fingerprints. "Johnny—"

"What's wrong, Kim?"

A sliver of guilt bled through Kim at his distressed tone. She hated to disturb him when he and Rachel were just getting settled in. "Someone broke into the cabin tonight."

Johnny made a shocked sound. "Are you and Lucy all right?"

Tears pricked Kim's eyes as she saw Brandon scrape a hand through his thick, wavy dark hair. "Yes. I called for Brody, but he wasn't there. Brandon answered and came over."

"Brandon's there with you?"

"Yes."

"Thank God."

Kim breathed in and out to wrestle her emotions under control. She'd relied on Johnny for so long she didn't know how not to. He was the only one she'd ever let down her guard around. He was the only one who knew the truth.

Johnny cleared his throat. "Kim, are you really okay?"

His words hung in the air. He was referring to the fact that she'd seen Brandon face-to-face for the first time in years. "No…" She sucked in another breath. "But I will be. The sheriff's here now."

"Good."

She closed her eyes, reliving the nightmarish memory. "You should have called me and warned me about the prison break."

Johnny released a pent-up breath. "I'm sorry. I only found out a couple of hours ago. I was going to call you in the morning."

"Do you think Carter came here tonight?" Kim asked. "That he was the intruder?"

A heartbeat of silence passed, riddled with anxiety. "I don't know, but sooner or later he'll show up at your place, or mine or Brandon's. And he'll want to see Lucy."

"So he knows about her?"

"He had the newspaper with the photos of the rodeo the last time we talked." Johnny paused. "He probably thinks you'll be more willing to help him than Brandon or me."

"I don't know," Kim said. "He was furious with me the last time we talked."

"I don't believe he'd hurt you, but he's in a bad way. We don't know what happened at the jail." He hesitated. "Still, I sure as hell don't want you to stay there tonight or to be alone until he's caught. Pack Lucy up and drive to my place. Or if you're too shaken up, I'll drive over and pick you up."

Kim shivered at the thought of staying in the cabin the rest of the night. But she'd vowed to let Johnny have his own life now. He had Rachel and Kenny, and she had to stop leaning on him.

"No, Johnny. I'll be fine here," she said instead.

"Kim—"

"Listen, big brother, I appreciate the fact that you care, but I'm a big girl now. I'm not going to horn in on you and Rachel every time some little problem occurs."

"Carter is not a *little* problem, Kim. He could be dangerous." Johnny paused, then lowered his voice. "There is another option, you know."

Kim leaned against the porch rail. She had a bad feeling he was going to want to post some goon on her. "I don't want a stranger in my house—"

"I'm not talking about hiring a bodyguard, Kim, although I can do that." He paused. "I think it's time you talk to Brandon."

A chill of foreboding rippled through her. "No, Johnny, I can't—"

"He'll protect you and Lucy, Kim, and you know it."

Her throat clogged. Yes, he probably would. But all the hurt and pain of the past would resurface. Just looking at him now, remembering how deeply she'd loved him and how heartbroken she'd been when he'd left her, robbed her breath.

She had dreamed of marrying him from the time she was fifteen years old.

But he'd taken another bride.

"Listen, sis, I understand this is difficult, and I know you were hurt and had your reasons for avoiding Brandon and for keeping secrets. But he's been divorced almost a year now, and he deserves to know the truth. So does Lucy—"

The sheriff walked out then, Brandon behind him, and she pressed her hand over the mouthpiece. "Hold on, Johnny."

"I'm taking off now, Ms. Long," Sheriff McRae said. "I'll let you know if we get any hits on the prints."

Kim thanked him, then looked up to see Brandon watching her.

"Is that Johnny?" Brandon asked.

Kim nodded, and Brandon reached for the phone. "Let me speak to him."

She moved her hand and spoke to her brother. "Brandon wants to talk to you, but Johnny—"

"Don't worry. I'm not going to tell him anything. That's up to you, Kim." Frustration laced her brother's voice. "But like I said, it's time you two talked. You owe it to Lucy."

Kim swallowed a retort and handed Brandon the phone, then inched closer to the doorway to check on Lucy again. Thankfully, she was still sleeping.

Was Johnny right? Was it time for her to confess to Brandon?

But what if she told him and he tried to take Lucy from her? He had money now....

"Johnny...yeah..." Brandon cut his gaze toward her, a dozen emotions flitting across his rugged face. The scar on his forehead he'd gleaned from one of his daddy's beatings puckered as he frowned. "Don't worry. I'll be ready if he shows up."

He disconnected the call, then handed Kim the phone. The simple brush of his fingers across hers sent a bolt of desire through her.

She jerked the phone to her and closed her hand around it, praying he hadn't seen her reaction as she stepped into the den.

"Pack a bag for you and Lucy," Brandon said, following her inside. "You're going to my place for the night."

Panic streaked through Kim. "I don't think that's a good idea, Brandon."

His jaw hardened, the vein at the base of his neck throbbing the way it always had when he was trying to control his anger. "This is not up for debate. I told Johnny I'd take you two to my ranch so you'd be safe for the night, and I intend to keep my word."

Their gazes locked, and she remembered other promises he'd made to her. One in particular. The night they'd first made love, he'd promised to love her and take care of her forever.

A promise he hadn't kept.

Was he remembering that, too?

"I'll talk to Johnny—"

"I'm not arguing." He jerked his thumb toward the house. "You either pack a bag, or I'll do it for you."

Kim had forgotten how bullheaded Brandon could be. That when he set his mind to something he charged after it and refused to let anything or anybody stand in his way.

Just like he had when he'd decided to better himself and buy his own ranch. Not that that had been a hard choice. Ranching was in his blood just as it was her brother's and in hers. But with his awful childhood, he hadn't had it easy. In fact the cards had been stacked against him.

Old hurts stabbed at her. She'd wanted them to work together to build a home and a ranch. But he'd chosen Marty to do those things with.

No. There was no way she could spend the night in Brandon's house, not in the place he'd shared with his wife.

"I appreciate the offer, Brandon, but you can't tell me what to do anymore. Lucy and I will be fine here."

Anger flashed in his eyes. "You'd rather face Carter alone if he returns?"

At this point, she didn't know if she was more afraid of Carter or Brandon. Carter had a temper, and if he was coming for Lucy and she opposed him, he might hurt her. After all, he'd had five long years for his anger to fester.

But he didn't have the power over her that Brandon had.

Then again, she didn't know how Brandon would react when he finally learned the truth about Lucy.

He had a bad temper, too. And now he had money and power....

"Please, just go, Brandon. I've taken care of Lucy all these years by myself. I can do it now."

He twisted his mouth sideways the way he used to do when he was working his thoughts to make a point. "Really? Then you and Lucy have visited Carter?"

She shook her head. "No." Carter hadn't wanted to see her. And jail was no place for a little girl.

Brandon gripped her arms. "Then he's not going to be happy with you when he arrives, is he?" Brandon's gruff voice rose a notch, and Lucy suddenly stirred.

"Mommy?" Lucy rolled over and looked at them. Her eyes widened with fear at the sight of Brandon gripping her arms. "Don't hurt my mommy!"

She jumped off the sofa and threw herself at Brandon, slamming her fists into Brandon's legs. "Stop it, don't hurt my mommy!"

BRANDON'S HEART CLENCHED at the terror in the little girl's cries, and he immediately released Kim. Dear God, Lucy thought he was going to hit her mother.

Shame engulfed him, memories of his own childhood flashing back. His daddy beating his mama. His sister's screams of terror. Him in the middle, trying to protect them both.

Kim stooped down to pull Lucy away. "It's okay, Lucy. He wasn't hurting me."

"But he yelled at you." Lucy's lower lip trembled as Kim picked her up; then she rubbed her teary eyes and looked up at Brandon.

Brandon forced his hands to hang limply by his sides, determined to prove to the child that he wouldn't hurt her or her mother.

But his chest clenched when he looked into Lucy's big green eyes.

Pale green eyes that looked just like his own.

He staggered back, shock bolting through him as the truth hit him.

Lucy wasn't Carter's little girl.

She was his.

Chapter Three

The truth echoed in Brandon's head over and over as if he'd been sucker punched.

Lucy was his.... Lucy was his.... He had a daughter....

A daughter he'd never known about.

Because Kim had kept it from him.

The anguish and rage hit him so hard that Brandon staggered backward, then gripped the sofa edge to keep from reaching for Kim and shaking her. How could she have done this to him?

For years he'd forced himself to accept the fact that he'd never have a family. Never have a son or daughter of his own because he was too afraid he'd pass on that horrific genetic disorder. Krabbe's Leukodystrophy, the doctor called it. The bone marrow transplant had miraculously given her a few extra years, but she had still suffered.

And for four years now, he'd had a living, breathing little girl who was his blood kin. A *normal* child.

One he'd made with Kim.

A child he would have loved and spoiled and been there for if only Kim had let him.

Bitterness filled him, and he fisted his hands by his

sides, his body trembling with the effort to control his anger.

Kim cradled Lucy to her as if she sensed that rage, as if she feared he was going to snatch her away. But her eyes also flashed with resignation as if she'd known this moment would eventually come and had dreaded it.

"Brandon—"

Their gazes locked, the air vibrating with the cloying scent of lies. "She's m—"

Kim cut him off with a choked whisper. "Yes."

That one word ripped a hole in his heart. "How could you?" he asked through gritted teeth. "Why?"

"You… We…" She nodded toward Lucy, her voice quavering. "This is not the time to discuss it, Brandon."

Dammit, it sure as hell was time to discuss it. It was *past* time. Fury surged through him, more powerful than he'd ever felt. He wanted to shout at Kim and demand to know how she could have left him in the dark about his own child.

He wanted to pull Lucy into his arms and hug her and make up for lost time.

But Lucy clawed at her mother in fear, and he forced himself to temper his reaction.

Still, his heart was pounding, and he had to clear his throat twice to make it work. "You kept this from me all these years and now you don't want to talk about it?"

Even though he'd tried, his voice still sounded harsh and loud in the hollow silence, and Lucy whipped her little head around, her eyes startled, scared.

His gut tightened with remorse. The poor little girl, *his* little girl, had been terrified of an intruder, and now he was adding to her fears.

He took a step forward, aching to drag her in his

arms and hold her, to assure her that he would never hurt her. That he hadn't been around the past four years because he hadn't known she was his. That he would love her and take care of her and tuck her into bed at night and teach her to ride, and be the father he should have been all along.

If Kim hadn't deprived him of it.

Images of the years he'd missed crawled through his mind, a blinding haze of pictures of Lucy. Lucy as a newborn swaddled in a pink blanket, her first laugh, the day she'd learned to crawl, her first step, then birthdays and Christmases—all memories Kim had that he'd missed.

God, what had she told Lucy about him?

"Mommy?" Lucy said in a frightened whisper.

Kim held her daughter tight, gently rocking Lucy in her arms. "It's okay, sugar. This is Johnny's friend Brandon. Remember, you watched him do trick riding at the rodeo and wanted to learn to ride like him?"

Lucy nodded, but her wide-eyed look made Brandon feel like the worst kind of heel.

And resurrected memories of how terrified his own sister had been of their father.

He'd sworn that if he ever had a child, a family, they would never be afraid of him.

But Lucy was.

Nausea gripped him, and he tore himself away and strode out onto the front porch. Aching inside and calling himself a hundred kinds of a fool, he leaned against the porch rail and dragged in the fresh air, desperate to stem the bile clogging his throat.

Was that the reason Kim had kept Lucy from him? Had she feared he'd be violent like his old man?

He closed his eyes, the image of Kim's tears the day

he'd broken up with her haunting him. He'd loved her but decided he could learn to love Marty. Marty was his ticket to the big time, to raising himself from trailer trash to a respected ranch hand to eventually owning his own spread. He'd been stupid and chosen wrong because he thought Marty would give him his future.

But in the end, he had been the one to lose.

His future had been with Kim and the child she'd been carrying. Only he hadn't known it.

Her words taunted him. *"This is Brandon, Uncle Johnny's friend."*

Hell, he was way more than Uncle Johnny's friend.

He was Lucy's daddy. And now he knew about her, he would be a father to her.

Even if he had to fight Kim to do so.

KIM SANK ONTO THE SOFA hugging Lucy to her. She hated the devastation she'd seen in Brandon's eyes. Pain she'd put there by her lies.

But he had left her and married another woman. And she had tried to tell him about Lucy, but...

"Mommy?" Lucy murmured. "I'm sweepy."

Lucy's words jerked her back to the reality of the night and the break-in. She needed to put Lucy back to bed. They both needed rest.

She listened for Brandon's car engine and expected him to peel away in a fit of anger, but didn't hear it. Instead her own breathing rattled, fraught with emotions.

How would she sleep tonight knowing someone had been inside the cabin? That it might or might not have been Carter?

Worse, how would Carter react if he thought Lucy

was his child, showed up expecting to see her and discovered she wasn't?

Not that she'd ever given him any reason to believe Lucy was his daughter. In fact, after their last confrontation when she'd visited him in prison, she hadn't had any communication with him.

But if he'd seen their picture in the paper like Johnny said, he could have jumped to conclusions.

Suddenly footsteps pounded the porch, and Brandon reappeared at the door. Lucy's head shot up again, and she dug her nails into Kim's shoulders. Kim tried to stifle her own tremor as Brandon's bitter look pierced her.

"I need to put Lucy back to bed," Kim said. "We can talk tomorrow."

"You're not staying here," Brandon said, his jaw clenched. "Pack a bag for you and Lucy. You're both coming to my ranch."

Kim's lungs begged for a breath. The last place she wanted to be was at his house.

"We'll be fine here," Kim said. "Please, Brandon—"

Brandon strode past her into her bedroom and Kim followed. When he opened her closet door, she stepped in front of him. "Brandon—"

Lucy made a whimpering sound, and Brandon looked tormented as he lifted a hand and gently patted her back.

"It's okay, Lucy," Brandon said in a low, soothing tone. "I just want to keep you and your mother safe."

"But you're mad at Mommy," Lucy said, her lower lip trembling. "I don't wants to go if you're mad and gonna yell."

Brandon sucked air through his teeth, and Kim knew she had to do something to diffuse the situation. Brandon was stubborn, but he'd bent over backward to take care of his younger sister. He'd fended off bullies, taken beatings from their father to protect her, even fed her when she was sick.

He would want to get to know Lucy now.

How could she deny him his own little girl? Even though he'd broken her heart, he was a good, honorable, hardworking man. Now he'd made his wealth, he'd joined Johnny and Brody Bloodworth and several other wealthy ranchers to create the Bucking Bronc Lodge and help troubled kids.

And he was Lucy's father.

She didn't want her daughter to be frightened of him.

Besides, earlier, hadn't she worried about how much Lucy was going to miss Johnny, how much she'd missed by not having a father around?

Kim rubbed circles on Lucy's back. "You know how Uncle Johnny's voice gets loud sometimes when he's worried?"

Lucy nodded, a lock of her dark red hair falling across one damp cheek.

"Well, Brandon is just worried about us now. He wants us to spend the night with him so he can make sure that man who broke in doesn't come back." Although for all she knew Carter might show up at Brandon's.

But at least they would be able to deal with him together.

Maybe going with him was the wise thing to do.

She would just have to keep up her guard. If Brandon wanted to know why he'd missed the first four years of his daughter's life, she'd tell him the truth.

He had made that choice, not her. Now he'd have to live with it.

THE NEED TO HOLD LUCY was so strong that it nearly overpowered Brandon. But he forced himself to summon every ounce of restraint he possessed and simply watch as Kim deposited Lucy onto her bed and began to pack.

Lucy cradled her stuffed lamb to her like a lifeline, and memories flooded him. When his sister Joanie had been ill or had nightmares, he'd rocked her to sleep. And when she'd grown into a preteen and it seemed inappropriate for him to cradle her in his lap, he'd sat by her bed and read to her and told her stories about riding and adventures they would take one day.

Each day though, he'd seen her grow physically weaker and more mentally impaired until finally he'd been forced to seek help. Without the money to pay for private care, he'd had to send her to a group home.

Leaving her there had damn near killed him.

He'd vowed one day to make enough money to bring her home and hire a nurse, one of the main reasons he'd married Marty Canterberry. But Joanie had died before he'd earned enough money to fulfill his promise.

And now he had all the money he needed, but an empty house and an empty life.

Except for the boys at the BBL.

You have a little girl.

A beautiful little girl with Kim's striking dark red hair and his green eyes. A little girl with crooked teeth and dimples and freckles—a perfect child.

For a moment, he couldn't breathe again. Instead, he said a silent prayer of thanks to God. Why He'd given Brandon this chance to be a father when the odds had been stacked against him he didn't know.

But he'd damn well do everything in his power to make the good Lord proud.

Kim fastened her suitcase, then rubbed a hand across Lucy's hair. Her eyes were heavy with sleep, her heart-shaped face angelic.

"I'm going to pack you a bag now, honey. You can stay here. I'll be right back."

Lucy nodded, and Brandon felt as if Kim had given him a small gift by trusting him with their daughter while she packed.

"You're really Uncle Johnny's friend?" Lucy asked in a tiny whisper.

Brandon eased closer and sat down on the edge of the bed, careful not to startle her. "Yes, I grew up with your uncle and your mom. We all played together when we were kids. We even built a fort and called it our secret meeting place."

Her eyes perked up with interest. "I wants a fort."

Brandon blinked back emotions. Was Lucy a tomboy like Kim had been? "Tell you what, sweetie, we'll build you one at my ranch. I'll even let you pick out the spot. How does that sound?"

He tweaked her nose, and an excited smile curved her rosebud of a mouth.

"Good." Lucy sighed sleepily.

Brandon soaked in the moment, memorizing the details of her face. Tiny freckles dotted her pug nose, and her long auburn lashes curled against her baby-soft skin. She had a quirky little mouth like Kim, and a defiant stubborn chin like his.

"You got horses?" Lucy asked on a yawn.

"Yes, ma'am, I sure do," Brandon said. "Maybe you can sleep in the car on the way, and in the morning I'll show you around and you can pick out which horse you want to be your own." He patted her foot. "Would you like that?"

She bobbed her head up and down. "Uh-huh…" Her voice faded as her eyes drifted closed.

But he could have sworn the smile stayed tucked in place, as if she was dreaming about an Appaloosa or palomino and the fort they would build.

He filed the moment away in his mind to treasure forever. One of the first memories in a lifetime of endless ones to come, he hoped.

Kim returned a second later with a small pink rolling bag and a backpack in the shape of a bunny rabbit and set them on top of her suitcase. "I still don't think this is a good idea."

Her wary expression infuriated him, but he tempered his tone. "It doesn't matter if you like it or not, Kim. Keeping Lucy safe is my job now, and I'm not going to let her down."

Anguish flickered in her eyes and something akin to fear followed, but he didn't take time to analyze it. He yanked up both suitcases to carry to his SUV. "I'll be back to get Lucy."

"No, I'll carry her." Kim leaned over to pick up her daughter, but Brandon caught her arm.

"You may not think much of me, Kim. And God knows, my old man was vile. But I'm not like him. I would never hurt Lucy."

Her stunned eyes met his, the wariness dissipating. "I…know that, Brandon."

His throat thickened, making his voice sound like he'd swallowed gravel. "That's not the reason you kept her from me?"

She shook her head. "God, no…. I…would never think that."

For a second, he couldn't speak. It was as if they had

stepped back in time to a moment when she trusted him and he trusted her, and their love had sparked to life.

Then he looked down at Lucy again and an image of her as a baby taunted him, hammering home the reality of the years he'd missed, and anger surged through him again.

Exhaustion lined Kim's face as she leaned over to scoop up Lucy, and concern for her and the ordeal she'd been through tonight suffused him. They needed to get on the road so she and Lucy could rest.

So he relented and carried the suitcases to his SUV, then opened the back door for Kim to settle Lucy in the back. Kim secured the seat belt. Then he returned to the cabin and grabbed a couple of pillows to make Lucy's ride more comfortable while Kim retrieved her purse and phone.

Kim settled into the front seat without saying a word, and he cranked the engine and headed down the drive away from the ranch. He was desperate for a confrontation, but bit his tongue.

They would have heated words, and he didn't intend to become his father and subject Lucy to his wrath. He didn't want to scare her again.

He punched in the sheriff's number before they made the turn-off onto the main road from the Bucking Bronc Lodge toward San Antonio.

"Sheriff, it's Brandon Woodstock. Kim Long and her daughter are going to my ranch until you find the person who broke in."

"Fine. You heard from your buddy Carter?"

"No," Brandon said. "But I'll let you know if I do."

When he disconnected, Kim was watching him with that wary look again.

"I need to call Johnny and tell him where we are."

He slanted her a dark look. "Johnny knows about Lucy?"

Kim twisted her hands together, then gave a slow nod. "Brandon—"

"Don't," he said sharply. Pain knifed through him again. Betrayal at its worst. The two people he'd loved more than his own life had both lied to him for years. "There's nothing you can say that will make what the two of you did to me right."

Then he shut down. He'd had more emotional upheaval today than he'd had in years. The weight of it was choking him. Part of him wanted to roll up and die.

But then Lucy shifted in the backseat, and he saw her tiny reflection in the rearview mirror, and for the first time in years, he realized he had something important to live for. Someone more important than himself or his goals.

He had a little girl.

Love mushroomed inside him, filling him with a kind of deep-seated joy that he'd never experienced.

Out of the corner of his eyes, he caught Kim's troubled expression, but he couldn't reach out to her or forgive her, so he let the silence between them fall.

By the time they'd passed through San Antonio and sped down the long deserted stretch of country road leading to his ranch, fatigue had claimed Kim and she'd fallen asleep. Occasionally he noticed a few cars passing, one behind him in the distance, then a trucker on a late run.

But a few more miles down the road, as the scrub brush, cacti and pastureland took over and the houses and buildings of San Antonio faded into the dust, he noticed headlights behind him. Distant hills outlined the horizon, the sky an inky well with a quarter moon sitting low over the tops of the mesquite and juniper trees.

The sound of an engine speeding up broke the silence. Then tires squealed and he tensed as he realized the vehicle was bearing down on him. Was it a cop?

He checked his speedometer. He hadn't been speeding. And it was the middle of the night. Maybe the cop was on his way to an accident somewhere, but there were no blue lights or a siren.

Then suddenly the vehicle shot forward, gaining on him fast.

Brandon frowned. Was it Carter? Could he have stolen a truck and followed them from Kim's?

He accelerated and rounded a curve, careful to keep the SUV on the road. He had precious cargo inside.

But the truck raced forward, swerving left, then right, then zoomed up beside him and skimmed his side just as he neared the ravine. Sparks flew from the guardrail and his truck. Gripping the steering wheel to keep the SUV on the road, he lifted his foot off the gas, hoping the truck would pass. Instead, the driver suddenly swerved a hard right toward him and rammed his side.

Sweat beaded on his skin as the SUV lurched out of control. Kim jerked awake, startled.

"Brandon?"

"Hang on," he said between gritted teeth.

The truck rammed them again, Kim cried out in shock and the SUV hit the side of a piney oak, spit gravel, then began to spin, fishtailing back and forth, skidding toward the ravine.

Chapter Four

Kim screamed as the truck skidded across the asphalt and Lucy jerked awake.

"Mommy!" Lucy cried.

"Hang on, honey," Brandon said in a gruff voice.

Tires squealed, and the gears made a grinding noise as the truck's headlights beamed across the ravine.

Kim clenched the dashboard to brace herself. They were going to crash!

Brandon threw out an arm to protect her as the truck spun a hundred and eighty degrees. Headlights pierced the darkness from an oncoming car and the vehicle that had slammed into them screeched past, flying down the road.

Brandon swerved closer to the ditch to avoid hitting the oncoming car, hanging on to the steering wheel to control the truck as it careened to a stop. They nose-dived into the embankment, but he managed to miss going into the ravine by just a few inches.

"Mommy!" Lucy cried again.

Kim pivoted to check on her daughter. "Lucy, are you okay?"

Lucy tried to unfasten her seat belt. "What's wrong?"

"Sorry, honey, I had to stop fast to keep from hitting

that other car." Brandon cut the engine and glanced at Kim worriedly. "Are you all right, Kim?"

She dragged in a labored breath but nodded. Brandon twisted around, clicked open Lucy's seat belt, then helped Lucy crawl over the seat into Kim's lap. Kim wrapped her arms around her daughter, battling tears as her gaze locked with Brandon's.

Moonlight streaked the window, highlighting his wide strong jaw and troubled eyes.

"Brandon," she whispered. "Who was that?"

"I don't know," he murmured. Then he drew her and Lucy into his arms, buried his head against them and held them. His breathing was ragged, and a fine tremor ran through him as he pressed a kiss into Lucy's hair.

A kiss that broke her heart for him and for Lucy and all they had missed.

Guilt tugged at her, but the old hurts resurfaced. Brandon had made that choice, not her.

Still, the events of the night flashed back in a terrifying rush. The break-in. Now the accident.

Only had it been an accident? It seemed like that car had intentionally hit them.

Another shudder whipped through her, and Kim couldn't help herself. She relaxed in Brandon's strong embrace, welcoming his comfort.

Even if he hated her for keeping his daughter from him the past four years, he would protect her and Lucy.

But questions plagued her. Who had been driving that truck? Carter?

Had he tried to kill them to get revenge because they hadn't helped him years ago?

BRANDON CLOSED HIS EYES, desperate to steady his pounding heart. What the hell was going on? First the break-in, now a hit-and-run?

They had to be connected.

Had Carter done this?

Surely he wouldn't have slammed into them with Lucy in the car. Carter had a mountain of pent-up anger and bitterness, but the man he'd once known had a soft spot for kids.

Unless he'd just figured out that Lucy wasn't his, that she was Brandon's daughter.

Still…

The sound of another car zooming by made him whip his head up. What if the driver of that damn truck returned?

His stomach knotted as he checked the road. But a sports car raced past as if it hadn't even seen them.

Lucy wiggled beneath his embrace, and as much as Brandon hated to let them go, he realized he was smothering them, and that they needed to get back on the road.

If that had been an intentional attack, they were sitting ducks out in the open like this.

So he slowly released them, and forced a calmness to his voice that he didn't feel. "Everybody okay?"

Kim's eyes still held a hint of fear, but she nodded. "Sure, we're tough girls, aren't we, Lucy?"

Lucy's lower lip quivered as she looked up at her mother, then at Brandon. But she raised her little chin and nodded.

Brandon's heart melted. "Well, then let's go." He tweaked Lucy's nose. "Think you can crawl into your seat and go back to sleep?"

"I don't know," she said, still clinging to Kim.

"Sure you can," Kim said with a smile. "And when you wake up, we'll be at Brandon's ranch."

Brandon gently stroked Lucy's hair. "I have a big bed your mama can tuck you into, and you can sleep as late as you want, and then we'll have my famous cinnamon toast and look at the horses."

Lucy studied him for a moment, her pale green eyes so like his own and his sister's that he couldn't drag his gaze away.

He'd protect her or die trying.

KIM WAS AFRAID Lucy might not fall back asleep, but she must have been exhausted because in minutes she was curled up with her blanket and stuffed animal again.

She wished she was as resilient. Between the break-in, hit-and-run and the tension between her and Brandon, she doubted she'd sleep another wink all night. Thankfully, Brandon hadn't pressed for more yet, but a confrontation was inevitable.

She stole a glance at him, and noticed his rigid posture. He kept checking the mirrors, and she realized he was staying alert in case that truck returned. The thought made her sit up straighter, and she stared out the window at the passing scenery searching the darkness.

As they passed long, flat stretches of wilderness dotted with desert cacti, creosote flats, yucca and cholla, then other ranches and farmland, her mind wandered to the day she discovered her pregnancy. She had only been eighteen, but she'd been so in love with Brandon that she would never have considered doing anything but raising her baby. She'd loved their child from the moment she'd found out she had conceived.

But Brandon had broken her heart a couple of months before and was on his honeymoon.

That had hurt the worst. To know that he was celebrating his love for another woman while she faced having a child alone. A child she'd desperately wanted to raise with him.

Her thoughts stayed scattered in the past as he veered onto a long winding road that looked at if it led nowhere. Moonlight streaked the horizon, painting a golden glow over the hills and valleys, and soon she saw cattle roaming and grazing in lush pastures.

He wound down a paved drive lined with billowing oaks that created a canopy above them, and she noted several barns, stables and riding pens.

Her pulse throbbed as they reached a stone wall, carved into an arch that held a wooden sign that said The Woodstock Wagoneer.

Brandon had talked and dreamed about owning his own spread when they were growing up, and she couldn't help but be proud that he'd accomplished it. And the name…something about it tickled her memory.

A romantic wagon ride they'd taken after prom…

No, he wouldn't have named the ranch The Wagoneer because of that ride. Would he?

Tears pricked her eyes again, but she blinked them away. Then she spotted a sprawling white farmhouse with gigantic wraparound porches, a white picket fence and dormer windows, and her heart stopped. Flower beds filled with pansies flanked the front porch and ferns hung from the awning, swaying in the breeze. Rocking chairs created a seating area near a porch swing like the Bucking Bronc Lodge, only not as rustic. This one was painted white with blue shutters.

Like the old abandoned farmhouse where they'd played as children.

Except this house wasn't old or abandoned. It looked exactly like the house she'd pointed to in a magazine one time when they'd been daydreaming.

She swung her gaze to Brandon's as he cut the engine, and for a moment, their gazes locked. Memories of all the times they'd laughed and loved and dreamed together flooded her. She'd fantasized about having a home like this.

But Brandon had built it for another woman.

Pain wrenched through her as if someone had driven a knife into her chest. She threw the door open, stumbled outside the car and gasped for air.

How could she stay here on Brandon's ranch knowing he had left her pregnant and alone while he built her dream home for another woman?

BRANDON GRITTED HIS TEETH as Kim climbed out. He hoped to hell she didn't remember the picture of the house she'd shown him years ago. If she did, she'd know that he'd built this house for her.

That he'd never gotten over her. That he'd regretted breaking her heart and marrying Marty.

That he'd blindly hoped that one day he might win her love and trust again. He'd even contemplated asking her to let him be a father to Lucy when he'd thought she was Carter's daughter.

How pathetic had he been?

All that time he'd tried to love another woman when Kim had been in his heart, and she had kept his child from him. Kim should have known that he would have moved hell or high water to come back to her if he'd known. That he would have sacrificed everything—

the money, the job, the hopes of his own spread—just to have a child when he thought that was the one thing he'd never have.

He glanced in the backseat and saw his sleeping daughter, and the anger over his loss nearly overpowered him. When he looked up at Kim, her face was ashen in the moonlight.

A myriad of emotions flashed across her face; then she opened the door to get Lucy.

"I'll get her," he said, knowing Kim was exhausted and he had a flight of stairs to climb to carry her to one of the guest rooms.

Kim shook her head. "No, just get the luggage."

"Stop arguing, Kim," Brandon said between clenched teeth. "You're dead on your feet. Just grab your purse and follow me."

He opened the back door to the car, then unfastened Lucy's seat belt and scooped his little girl into his arms. Love swelled in his chest as she snuggled up against him.

He swallowed hard, then led the way up the cobblestone steps to the wraparound porch. How many times had he sat in that porch swing and imagined Kim cuddled up beside him?

Fool. That's what he was.

When he reached the front door, Kim hesitated, and he juggled Lucy to one side and unlocked the door, then stepped inside. He wasn't much for decorating so the place seemed bare as he flicked on a light. It definitely needed a woman's touch.

But it was home, so he strode up the winding staircase. Kim followed, her sigh indicating her fatigue.

He shoved open the first door to the right and gestured inside. "There are two guest rooms," he said.

"You can stay in the first one nearest the stairs. I'll put Lucy in the one beside you. There's a bathroom in between."

Kim nodded, then walked with him to the second room, where he flipped on a lamp and headed toward the white four-poster bed. Foolish again. He'd let the store clerk talk him into it, saying female guests would like it. He'd thought of Joanie, who would have loved it, then a little girl that he'd never have, but he'd bought it anyway.

Kim rushed to the bed and turned down the lavender comforter, and he helped ease Lucy onto the bed. For a moment, he simply stood and looked at her, soaking in the fact that she was his child. Memorizing her face again as if he feared she was a mirage and might disappear in the night.

Finally he dragged himself away, then strode down the steps and returned a few minutes later. He dropped Kim's bag off in the first room, then took Lucy's little rollaway and bunny backpack and put them on the window seat in front of the dormer window in her room.

He hesitated, soaking up the sight of his daughter again, then watched Kim bend over and kiss Lucy on the forehead and tuck her in tight. He'd never thought he could feel so many emotions at once.

Love for Lucy. An instantaneous bond that overwhelmed him with the need to protect her and the desire to make up for all the time he'd lost.

Admiration for Kim because she obviously loved their daughter and was a wonderful mother.

Anger that he'd missed out on being with both of them.

Kim smoothed the covers down, then turned and

looked up at him, her eyes instantly wary. She looked exhausted, and for a brief moment, he wanted to give her a reprieve. To hold and comfort her and forget all the pain between them. All the bitterness that surfaced at the thought of her with Carter.

Of her and Johnny keeping his daughter from him.

He gestured toward the door. "Downstairs. We need to talk."

Kim bit her lip, then sighed and headed down the stairs. He followed her, then led her into the study and poured them both a drink.

He'd held his tongue during the drive.

But her reprieve was over.

He wanted answers, and he wouldn't sleep until he had them. His heart hardened.

Although even then, nothing Kim said could ever make things right again between them.

Chapter Five

Kim's hand trembled as she stared into the rich red wine. She took a sip, hoping it would calm her raging nerves. But her legs felt weak and the night's strain was wearing her down.

"Why, Kim? Why did you keep my daughter from me?"

The cold bitterness in Brandon's voice hit her like a punch in the stomach. But painful memories swirled around her, rousing her own anger.

She lifted her head, refusing to let him dump the blame on her. "Because you told me you didn't want me, remember? That you were in love with another woman? Then you married her two weeks later."

The whirlwind romance had been almost as shocking and hurtful as the breakup. She had spent a lifetime with Brandon, yet he'd fallen for Marty Canterberry in weeks.

The ice clinked in Brandon's glass as he choked down his drink. "That didn't give you the right to keep my child from me." Anger made his voice harsh. "To not tell me I was going to be a father."

Kim finished the wine, then set the glass down with a thud and folded her arms. "The day I found out I was pregnant, you were on your honeymoon with your bride. Where did you go, Brandon? The Bahamas? Bermuda? I forget." A trace of sarcasm laced her tone. "I didn't think either you or your *wife* would welcome me showing up announcing that I was carrying your child."

There, that was the cold hard truth. Let him deal with it.

Brandon clenched the glass so tightly she thought it was going to break. "You could have told me when I returned."

"Yeah, right. Let's see—when you were setting up house with Marty?" Kim barked a laugh. "You gave up any right to me or to Lucy when you chose her over me."

Brandon's eyes flared hot. "So you kept her from me out of revenge?"

"No," Kim said, shocked that he would think she was that vindictive. "*You* didn't want me, Brandon. I didn't fit into your future, your dreams anymore. I couldn't help you achieve the success you wanted." A tremor rippled through her as she unleashed on him. "I didn't think you would want a baby either. She would have messed up your plans, too."

She paced to the window and looked out at the stars and moon. Darkness bathed the property, outbuildings and pastures. Yet she imagined Brandon and Marty riding across the land with the wind in their faces, smiling as they approached the house, and bitterness heated her blood.

Dammit, maybe a part of her had wanted to get back at him. He'd broken her heart, destroyed her dreams and left her pregnant while he was off screwing another woman and climbing his way to the top.

Brandon's feet pounded behind her; then he swung

her around to look at him. A muscle ticked in his clenched jaw. "You knew how much I loved my sister, Kim. How scared I was of having a child with that genetic disorder."

Kim stiffened. "Yes, I knew. And believe me, I worried that Lucy would have problems." And she'd struggled over what she would do if she discovered her baby had inherited that disorder. "Johnny took me to a specialist and paid for tests—"

"Johnny," Brandon muttered beneath his breath. "I should have been the one there, Kim. Not Johnny." He squeezed her arms so tightly Kim winced. Then he seemed to realize it and released her. "Johnny should have told me."

"I made him promise not to," Kim said, refusing to allow him to blame her brother. She inhaled a deep breath, seething. "Besides, you keep forgetting that you broke up with me."

"Then you went straight to Carter's bed."

"That's not how it happened," Kim said in a tortured voice. "Besides, we've been over this before. It's not like my sleeping with Carter for one night should have mattered to you anyway. You were already in Marty's bed."

"If I'd known about Lucy—"

"What?" Kim shouted. "You would have changed your mind?" She shoved her face in his. "You're unbelievable, Brandon Woodstock. Do you remember the horrible things you said to me the last night we saw each other? You called me all kinds of hurtful names and said you hated me." She threw up her hands. "Knowing how you felt, how could I possibly have come to you with the news that I was pregnant?

You probably would have accused me of trying to trap you."

"But you didn't want that, did you?" Brandon said in a hoarse voice. "You didn't fight for me at all."

No, she'd been too crushed. And how could she have fought against Marty Canterberry, with her gorgeous body and social standing and money. She had everything Kim hadn't had.

And she had helped Brandon achieve his dreams.

"Don't you dare make this about me." Kim poked him in the chest. "You walked away, Brandon. You made your feelings about me clear back then. You made your choice. I had to live with it and now so do you."

She brushed her hands down her sides, determined to survive this confrontation with some dignity intact. "Now, I'm exhausted and Lucy will be up in the morning with a million questions. I'm going to bed."

"Wait a minute." Brandon pressed a hand to her shoulder as she tried to pass him, his voice low, his eyes tormented. "What did you tell Lucy about me, Kim?"

Kim's gaze met his. She wanted to lash out again, but instead she told him the truth. "I told her that her father was a great guy, but he couldn't be with us." Because he had another family.

"Well, I am here," Brandon said in a gruff voice. "And now that I finally know about her, I am going to be a part of her life whether you like it or not." He remained rigid, his breathing labored in the ensuing silence. "Either you tell her who I am in the morning or I will."

Kim froze. "Brandon, be reasonable. Let her get to know you—"

"I won't push her," Brandon said sharply. "But it's time she knows the truth."

The breath stalled in Kim's chest, her anxiety mounting as she twisted away from his hold. "Fine. I'll tell her. But Lucy is innocent in all this, Brandon. And if you bad-mouth me in front of her or frighten her, I will take her and leave."

She didn't wait for a reply. She turned and ran up the steps. Her chest was heaving for air as she shut the bedroom door and pulled on a sleep shirt.

Brandon owned one of the largest ranches in Texas and knew people everywhere. He had money and power, and he was angry.

What if he decided to strike back at her and demand to have Lucy on a permanent basis?

If it came down to a custody battle, she would fight him. Lucy was her life. She couldn't go on without her....

BRANDON POURED himself another Scotch, then walked over to the window and looked outside. God, what kind of person did Kim think he was? Did she really think he'd frighten Lucy or disparage her in front of their child?

You left her. You said horrible things the night you found out about Carter. And you frightened Lucy tonight when you yelled at Kim.

He choked down the drink.

Dammit, he'd made a mess of things. He had hurt Kim and ruined his own life by marrying Marty.

Sure, he'd earned his wealth and owned a spread to be proud of, a place that would make the kids who'd laughed and bullied him when he was younger envious as hell. Although both had come too late for Joanie.

And now…

Johnny. If only Johnny had told him the truth he would have done things differently. He didn't care what time it was. He picked up the phone and punched in his number. Johnny answered on the second ring.

"Brandon, is everything all right?" Fear roughened Johnny's voice. "Are Kim and Lucy okay?"

"They're fine."

"Where are you?"

"My place," Brandon said. "Although someone tried to run us off the road on the way here."

"What?" Johnny muttered. "Did you see the driver?"

"No. He hit us and raced on." Brandon paused. "It could have been a drunk driver or a teenager, but I have a bad feeling it was intentional."

"You mean Carter?" A noise sounded and Brandon realized Johnny was probably getting out of bed. "I can't believe he'd try to kill you, especially with Lucy in the car."

Brandon sucked air through his teeth. "Speaking of Lucy, why didn't you tell me about her, Johnny?"

A hiss sounded over the line. "It was Kim's secret to tell."

Emotions thickened Brandon's throat, betrayal at its worst. "But you were my friend, like family…" His voice cracked. "You knew about Joanie, that I would have loved Lucy."

He bowed his head into his hands, raw anguish seeping through him.

"Look, Brandon, you can be pissed off at me. And I guess you have a right to be mad at Kim. But you played a big part in this situation, so don't blame her without taking a good hard look at yourself."

"Dammit, Johnny—"

"And another thing," Johnny said, on a roll. "You may have missed out on the past four years, but you have no idea how difficult life has been for Kim. Watching you marry that other woman damn near killed her. She loved you and you crushed her and left her alone and pregnant."

Brandon cleared his throat. "But you know—"

"Yeah, yeah, you had your reasons. Dammit, Brandon, it doesn't matter." Johnny's sigh was steeped in anger. "What matters is that you have a second chance. A chance to make it up to Kim. And a chance to be the father Lucy deserves. So don't screw it up this time by harping on blame and bitterness. It will eat you up, just like it has Carter the past few years."

Brandon cursed. The last thing he expected from Johnny was a holier-than-thou lecture.

"It's late, and I'm going back to bed with Rachel. Kenny will be up early," Johnny said. "Call me if you hear from Carter or if he shows up. Meanwhile, keep my sister and niece safe or you'll answer to me."

Brandon gritted his teeth as the phone clicked into silence. Dammit, Johnny had hung up on him.

But his words echoed in Brandon's ears as he flipped off the light and headed into his bedroom. A gigantic suite that he slept in alone.

Brandon cursed again as he stripped off his jeans and shirt and fell into bed. He'd blown his chance with Kim long ago.

But Johnny was right about one thing. He had Lucy now. She would be up early in the morning, too, probably along with the sun.

He couldn't turn back time and rectify his mistakes.

But he could be the father Lucy hadn't had for the past four years.

KIM TOSSED AND TURNED, her thoughts ping-ponging back and forth between relief that her secret was finally out, dread over telling Lucy the truth, and anxiety over losing her daughter to Brandon.

It was too late for them to be a family

But she was so exhausted she finally fell into a deep and fitful sleep. She jerked awake twice, her heart pounding, and rushed to check on Lucy, but both times her daughter was snuggled deep in the plush covers of the four-poster bed, sleeping like an angel.

She had no idea that her world was about to change.

For a moment, Kim simply watched Lucy sleep, wishing she could freeze time and keep her innocent and young forever. Then her gaze skimmed over the room.

The feminine décor made her wonder if it had been designed for a little girl. Had Brandon and Marty decorated the room for a child they planned to have?

Hurt stabbed her at the thought, but she was too tired to dwell on it, so she stumbled back to bed. Finally exhaustion claimed her and she dozed to sleep.

The next time she awakened, sunlight streamed through the window, bright and warm. When she glanced at the clock, she was surprised it was almost eight o'clock.

She raced through the bathroom to the adjoining room and froze at the sight of the empty bed.

Where was her daughter? Had Brandon already spilled the truth?

Her pulse clamored as she threw off her nightshirt, dragged on a pair of jeans and T-shirt, then socks and boots. She tossed some cold water on her face, swiped a brush through her hair, then pulled it into a ponytail and hurried down the steps.

The scent of coffee and cinnamon wafted toward her, and she followed the smell to the kitchen. But Brandon and Lucy weren't inside.

A tray of cinnamon toast sat on the stove, two empty plates stacked in the sink. Brandon and Lucy had obviously shared breakfast together—without her. Her heart wrenched. Was that the way it would be? Brandon would slowly ease his way into Lucy's life, then convince her to come and live with him?

No, she wouldn't allow it.

Where were they now?

She grabbed a hand-painted Native American mug from the stand on the counter, poured herself a cup of coffee, then glanced out the window to see if she spotted them. Horses galloped in the pasture across the path and cows grazed in the fields, the sun shimmering off of golden blades of freshly cut spring grass. She glanced around the kitchen and noted the blue and white tiles and old-fashioned whitewashed pie safe, a memory tickling her consciousness.

The kitchen in the photo she'd shown Brandon had been blue and white. And she'd told him she wanted a pie safe because her grandmother used to have one. She'd bake apples and sit them on it to cool in the afternoon, filling the house with the wonderful, homey smell.

It was one of the few good childhood memories she had. Other than playing with Johnny and Brandon and Carter.

Yet once again, she realized he'd built this house, the one of her dreams, for his wife.

A noise outside jerked her from her reverie and to the present, and panic stabbed at her again.

She clutched the coffee in one hand, then walked outside the kitchen door. A creaking sound caught her attention, and she turned toward it.

Her heart fluttered when she spotted Lucy and Brandon sitting in the porch swing. Brandon had his arm draped casually along the back of the swing, pushing it back and forth with one leg while Lucy chattered away.

"When can we see the horses?" Lucy asked. "You said I could pick one to wide."

So like Lucy. She never forgot a promise.

"Soon," Brandon said with a smile in his tone. "We'd better wait on your mom. She might worry if she woke up and we were gone."

Kim sipped her coffee, relieved at his comment.

"Here she comes now," Brandon said, the lightness fading from his voice as he met her gaze.

"You was a lazy bones, Mommy," Lucy said with a giggle. "We already had bweakfast! Mr. Bwandon made cinmon toast."

Kim smiled. "I know. I smelled it all the way up the stairs."

Lucy kicked her legs back and forth rocking the swing. "Mr. Bwandon said we had to wait on you to look at the horsies. I wants to go now."

Kim sank into one of the rocking chairs. The sight of Brandon and Lucy swinging together was so sweet that it nearly brought tears to her eyes. "Hang on a second, and he can show us around the ranch together."

"No, now," Lucy said, crossing her arms in a pout.

"Let your mother finish her coffee first." Brandon leaned forward with his elbows on his knees. "Besides, we have something to tell you."

Lucy squinted up at him, her eyes huge. "What? Is it about that bad man last night?" Lucy twisted her stuffed lamb's ear. "Is he comin' here?"

"No, baby," Kim said, hoping she was right. That the hit-and-run had been a drunk driver or some wild kids, not the intruder from the Bucking Bronc.

"It's about you and your mommy," Brandon said. "And me."

A frown puckered Lucy's dark red brows.

Kim glanced at Brandon, hoping for a reprieve, but determination flared in his eyes. A warning look. If she didn't tell Lucy, he would.

"Remember when you asked me about your daddy?" Kim asked softly.

Lucy toyed with the lamb's ear, then gave a small wary nod. "You said he couldn't be with us cause of his other famiwy."

"Yes, that's right," Kim said softly. "But now…well, now he's here, and he wants to see you and spend time with you."

Confusion marred Lucy's face, and she whirled around in the swing as if looking for her father. "Where is he?"

Kim patted Lucy's hand. "Sweetie, he's right beside you. Mr. Brandon…he's your father, honey."

Lucy crinkled her nose. "You're my daddy?"

Brandon swallowed, a dozen emotions brimming in his eyes. "Yes, Lucy. I'm your father."

A heartbeat of silence passed. Then Lucy's chin wobbled and a tear trickled down her cheek.

Kim reached out and wiped away the tear. "Lucy, honey, what is it? What's wrong?"

Lucy pinned Brandon with an accusatory look. "You

wiked your other famiwy more than us." She jutted up her chin in that defiant stubborn tilt. "So why do you wants to see us now?"

BRANDON'S CHEST CLENCHED. Johnny had given him a tongue-lashing, but he hadn't expected one from his young daughter.

What did you expect? That she'd jump into your arms and say she loved you? She doesn't even know you.

Which was Kim's fault.

And maybe...maybe a little bit yours...

He forced himself to keep his voice low. "I want to see you because I love you."

Lucy's eyes narrowed, and he realized she was a perceptive, smart little girl. She reminded him so much of Kim when she was little. The very reason he'd fallen in love with her.

"But you wiked your other famiwy the bestest?"

He froze, for the first time in his life at a loss for words. The truth was far too complicated for a four-year-old to understand. Hell, he didn't completely understand how he could have made the choices he'd made.

Except he'd given up the best thing in his life.

The best two things, he silently corrected himself. Only he hadn't been aware of the second.

Kim traced a finger around the edge of the coffee mug. He wanted her to help him out, but he'd dug this hole and he'd have to dig his way out.

"It's not like that," Brandon said quietly. "Your mom and I, we just made mistakes."

Another tear slipped down her cheek. "Like me? I did somfin wong?"

"No, honey, no." God, he was making a mess of this. He glanced at Kim and saw tears in her eyes, too. He had let them both down so badly.

How could he ever win Kim's trust again?

And his daughter—would he be able to win her love?

Chapter Six

Kim's heart ached at Lucy's words. Her gaze locked with Brandon's, and she saw him struggling as well. He hadn't meant to make Lucy feel that she was a mistake, but a four-year-old's mind pieced things together in its own mysterious way. And Lucy was intuitive. No telling what she'd heard from other kids at preschool or at the Bucking Bronc.

She clasped Lucy's hand. "No, Lucy, you didn't do anything wrong, honey. That's not what B— Your father meant."

Brandon gently brushed Lucy's hair from her cheek. "As a matter of fact, you are the most perfect little girl in the world. And I'm very proud to be your daddy."

Lucy wrinkled her nose. "But you wiked the other mommy bestest." She scooted away from him and clung to Kim's hand.

Brandon's expression turned pained. Kim didn't want to hear the answer. She already knew it.

"Lucy, honey—"

"Lucy, listen to me," Brandon said firmly. "Your mommy is the best mother in the whole world."

Lucy studied him warily for a long minute, then nodded and relaxed slightly.

His gaze cut to Kim's, condemning. "I'm sorry I wasn't around before." Regret underscored his voice. "But we're here together now." Brandon stroked her cheek with the pad of his thumb. "I'm going to be your daddy forever."

Lucy glanced at Kim for confirmation and Kim gave her a reassuring smile.

Then Lucy threw her arms around Brandon and squeezed his neck. "'Kay, Daddy. Now can we pwease, pwease, pwease go see the horsies?"

Brandon chuckled, but his face looked strained, and tears pricked Kim's eyes. She wanted Lucy to have a father, and she wanted Brandon to love their daughter.

She only wished that things between them hadn't gone so terribly wrong. That he could love her and they could be a family. But that could never happen. Too much heartache lay between them.

She would have to settle for watching him love Lucy. And somehow they would learn to work together so Lucy wouldn't be hurt when they left the Woodstock Wagoneer and returned to the Bucking Bronc Lodge.

"Why don't you run inside and potty and I'll grab a piece of toast?" Kim suggested. "Then Brandon can show us around and let you pick out that horse?"

"Yippee!" Lucy tumbled down from the swing, her red curls bobbing, then ran inside.

Brandon exhaled noisily and stood.

Kim cleared her throat. "Brandon, I know we've had our differences, but we can't put Lucy between us. We have to work together for her."

He clenched his jaw. "For once we agree."

Kim sighed, hoping they could actually bury their hostility, then hurried inside. Brandon followed and poured some coffee into a thermos.

Inside the kitchen, she grabbed a piece of toast and bit into it. The small TV was on, and a news flash beeped, drawing her attention.

"Yesterday three prisoners escaped from the state penitentiary, wounding a guard in their escape." Brandon walked up behind her, and they both watched as the reporter detailed the story.

"Joey Faradino, incarcerated for grand theft robbery, was originally from El Paso and may be headed back to that area. Robert Dugan was on death row for the brutal slaying of three women in west Texas, and is considered the most dangerous of the three felons." The reporter paused while photographs flashed on the screen.

"The third escapee was Carter Flagstone, who has been serving a life sentence for murder. An anonymous tip has come in saying Flagstone was seen on the outskirts of San Antonio late yesterday, and that he is considered armed and dangerous."

Kim shuddered at the photo of Carter that appeared. Even before prison, he'd looked worn down, hardened, his eyes defeated and cold. How would prison have changed him?

Brandon placed a hand at the small of her back. "He's close by, Kim."

A chill skated up her spine. "What if he followed us here?"

"It's possible." Brandon frowned. "In fact, he could already be hiding out on the ranch for all we know."

Kim clutched his arm, terrified. He was right. Carter could be hiding out on the property just waiting to get one of them alone. And if he'd tried to kill them last night, he might finish the job. "We have to watch

Lucy," Kim whispered. "We can't let her out of our sight."

Brandon's mouth thinned into a straight line. "Don't worry, Kim. If he wants Lucy, he'll have to kill me to get to her."

BRANDON UNDERSTOOD the fear in Kim's eyes.

Carter hated him. And if he believed Lucy was his daughter, and that Brandon was trying to move in on Kim or his child, he'd probably want revenge.

But Lucy bounced in, and a silent agreement passed between him and Kim. They wouldn't discuss Carter in front of Lucy. She had already been through enough the past two days.

Right now, he needed to make her feel safe and assure her that he loved her and would protect her.

And her mother.

"I wents potty. Weady to go?" Lucy asked.

Brandon chuckled. "Yep, let's do it."

Brandon and Kim walked out to his truck, Lucy skipping ahead. "First, I'll drive you around, then we'll stop at the riding stables," Brandon said as he swung Lucy into the backseat.

For the next hour he pointed out the sections of pastureland for his herd, and the stables and training pens for the quarter horses.

"I hired some ranch hands to help with the cattle, and trainers and groomers to work with the horses. Some of the employees live off the ranch, but a few stay in those cabins." He pointed at a row of cabins along the east ridge, then glanced at Kim. "You took a job at the Bucking Bronc, didn't you?"

"I figured it was time Lucy and I got out from Johnny's so he could have a life." Kim shrugged. "Besides, I finally earned my degree and figured I'd put it to use."

Brandon arched a brow. "Your degree?"

She nodded. "In counseling. Brody hired me to help train the horses but also to lead small groups and work with the boys." A frown darkened her face. "I hope we're back next week for the second camp."

He pressed his lips together but didn't comment. Kim always had been a sucker for a kid in need. God knows, she'd put up with him and Johnny and Carter.

"You train some of the horses yourself?" Kim asked.

Brandon shrugged. "Yeah. You know I'm a hands-on guy."

She twisted sideways, an odd look settling in her eyes.

"It's 'mongous!" Lucy said, then giggled when she spotted a baby calf wobbling toward the pond. Ducks and geese fluttered on the water and several Herefords had gathered for a drink.

"You mean *humongous,*" Kim said with a smile.

"That's what I said, 'mongous!" Lucy shouted.

Brandon chuckled. "Yeah, I've got five hundred acres. Sixty percent Hereford, forty percent Angus/Hereford and Brangus/Hereford cross."

"Your breeding business is prosperous," Kim said.

He gave her a sheepish look. "Yeah, it's been lucrative. And you know how much I like being in the saddle."

A blush stained her cheek for a second, and he remembered the times they had ridden together, her body rubbing his as she clasped her hands around his waist. Did Kim remember the good times, too? Or only that he'd dumped her?

They had finished the tour though so he parked at

the barn where he kept his favorite trail-riding horses. "Okay, kiddo," he said as he opened the back door and lifted Lucy down from the seat. "Now, the fun part."

Lucy squealed, her pigtails bobbing up and down as she disappeared inside. He and Kim followed, bypassing the tack room.

"This bay is mine," Brandon said as they stopped to pat a massive black stallion. "His name is Saint Salvador."

Lucy giggled as the animal nudged its nose into her palm and whinnied. The remaining horses in the barn caught on, each kicking and neighing and peering over the stall railings begging for attention.

Lucy stopped at the third stall and stared up in awe at his best tobiano paint.

"I wike this one!" she said, rubbing his nose. "He wooks wike a leopard!"

"That's because he's a paint," Brandon explained. "And an excellent choice, Lucy. He's very gentle."

Lucy wrinkled her nose. "Can I call him Spots?"

"Actually his name is Troubadour. But I think he'll like Spots better."

Kim grinned, and Brandon helped Lucy climb on the rail to see inside the stall.

Lucy clapped her hands. "Yippee! Now can we ride?"

"Let your mother make her selection," Brandon said. "Then we'll saddle up."

Brandon watched quietly as Kim made her way along the stalls. Just as he expected, Kim chose a palomino. He and Kim worked together to saddle the horses, once again reminding him of their youth. Although Kim was petite, she had a natural way with animals just as she did with kids.

She'd done a wonderful job raising Lucy.

But before they took a trail ride, Brandon led Spots into the pen and helped Lucy in the saddle. She squealed with delight as he led her around the pen.

"Let's go on the twails," Lucy said as she bounced up and down.

"Not yet," Brandon said. "First you and Spots have to learn to work together. He has to become comfortable with you, and you need to learn how to control and command him. You can ride on the back with me or your mom on the trail."

Lucy started to pout, but Brandon held firm, and Kim backed him up.

"Safety always comes first," Kim said. "But don't worry, Lucy. It won't take you and Spots long to become a team."

Brandon unsaddled Spots and showed Lucy how to brush her. Then they fed her and gave her water.

"I wants to ride on the back with you, Daddy," Lucy said as he led Saint Salvador from the stall.

Brandon glanced at Kim for approval, and she nodded, so he mounted then pulled Lucy up behind him.

When she wrapped her little arms around his waist, his heart swelled with love. As they rode across the pasture, he let himself imagine that they could be a family.

And for the first time since he'd bought the ranch, the place started to feel more like a home than a business.

TWO DAYS LATER, Kim sighed as she watched Brandon giving Lucy another riding lesson in the pen. He was a natural father, patient and attentive but firm, and he'd done everything possible to make her feel safe and protected, even cradling her the night before when she'd woken up screaming that a man was chasing her.

In fact, Lucy had turned to Brandon before her. A fact that hurt slightly, but how could she blame Lucy? Brandon was big and strong and tough, had always done everything to the extreme. And he'd always made her feel protected when she was young.

She leaned over the fence railing, reconciled to the fact that she and Brandon had to call a truce. Lucy adored her father.

Which would make it harder for them to leave, but sooner or later they had to. She wiped a smudge of dirt from her jeans. She and Brandon would arrange visitation, weekends, holidays, just as other couples who shared a child did.

Because her job at the Bucking Bronc Lodge was too important to her. It afforded her independence and fed her need to help others, and Lucy thrived around the other children.

Still, Lucy was getting attached to the Woodstock Wagoneer. The barn cat, Fifi, had had kittens, giving Lucy a thrill as she'd watched the mama deliver them. And, the night before, Brandon had driven them out to watch some of his hands herding cattle into the west pasture. Then Brandon had built a campfire outside, they'd roasted marshmallows, and he'd regaled Lucy with stories about how he and Johnny used to sneak onto the neighbor's ranch at night and chase the baby calves into the pond. How they'd hidden behind haystacks and studied the older ranchers breaking horses. How they'd slept on the ground and counted the stars and dreamed about owning their own ranches someday. And they'd taken odd jobs at a rodeo in exchange for learning trick riding and roping.

Lucy had been mesmerized by every word her father said.

Still, sometimes she feared she would lose Lucy to Brandon.

A truck rumbled in the distance, and her nerves instantly jerked to alert. They still hadn't heard from Carter, and neither had Johnny. It was just a matter of time before he surfaced.

He had nowhere else to go for help. Eventually he would turn to one of them. Either that or he'd come to exact revenge.

Brandon's cell phone jangled, and he answered. "Hello." A pause, then his smile faded. "Dammit. I'll be right there."

When he disconnected, he glanced at Kim. "Someone vandalized a couple of the barns on the west end. Probably some teenagers but I'd better check it out."

Kim nodded, opened the gate, then stepped inside and closed it. "Okay. Lucy and I will brush Spots down and feed her."

"Thanks." He gave Lucy a thumbs-up. "You did great today, honey. I'll be back in a little bit."

"Bye, Daddy!" Lucy waved, then urged Spots into a canter. "You did good today, too, Spots. We're a team now, aren't we?" The paint dropped his head forward and then threw it back as if he understood, and Lucy broke into giggles.

Kim helped her dismount; then they led Spots to the grooming platform. But as she and Lucy worked, worry needled her. What if the vandalism hadn't been teenagers?

What if it was Carter?

No...why would he vandalize the place? That would only draw attention to him. If he was hiding out on the ranch, that was the last thing he'd want.

The sun dipped lower in the sky, the spring air growing chilly by the time they led the paint into the stall.

Kim took Lucy's hand. "Come on, let's stir up some spaghetti sauce for dinner while we wait on your daddy." Just saying the word sent a pang of longing through Kim. Before she was even pregnant, she'd dreamed of having Brandon's baby and them being a family. And now they were.

Yet Brandon was committed to Lucy, he loved Lucy, not *her*.

In the kitchen, they washed up and Lucy helped add spices to the pot. Then Kim chopped fresh tomatoes, onions and herbs and sautéed some ground beef while Lucy drew a picture for her father at the kitchen table. Kim's heart tugged at the stick figures of Brandon and Lucy holding hands as they stood in the middle of a field of daisies beside Spots.

Already her daughter had fallen for her father.

She understood the feeling. But Brandon had crushed her years ago, and she couldn't allow herself to settle into a false sense of security and fall back in love with him.

Because he might break her heart all over again.

For all she knew, he and his wife might be planning a reconciliation.

That thought triggered a twinge of jealousy, but she squashed it. She had no claims on Brandon.

Only Lucy did.

What would Marty think if she knew they had a daughter? Where would Lucy fit in, especially if Marty demanded that he not see her?

Would Brandon give in and abandon Lucy as he had abandoned her years ago?

Anxiety knotted her stomach, and she set the sauce down to simmer and checked the clock. Where was Brandon? The vandalism must have been more serious than he'd thought....

"Mommy, can we play with the kitties before Daddy gets back?"

Kim sighed. "Sure, honey. I don't want to heat the bread until it's time to eat anyway."

She wrapped the bread in foil, then took Lucy's hand. Lucy tucked her lamb beneath one arm and they half skipped, half walked to the barn. Clouds had gathered from the east fighting with the moon for the sky, and the night seemed unusually dark and eerily quiet. In the distance, cows mooed, the sound of horses whinnying drifted in the wind, leaves rattled as the breeze picked up and insects buzzed and chirped.

A storm was brewing; she felt the hint of it in the air. Rain would be good for the grass, but thunderstorms always resurrected memories of her father's temper.

And the night she'd almost lost Lucy...

She banished the memory as they entered the barn and flipped on the light, but the light flickered on, then off, pitching them into darkness. Thunder rumbled outside, but Lucy seemed oblivious as she barreled inside. "Here, kitty, kitty, kitty..."

Lucy darted past the tack room toward the back stall where the mama cat had delivered, and Kim followed, but suddenly the barn door slammed shut behind them. Kim jerked around, but a sea of black clouded her eyes.

"Hello? Is someone there?"

The raspy silence that echoed back made her skin crawl. Anxious to get Lucy back to the house, she felt her way along the wall in the dark, wishing she'd brought a flashlight. Suddenly the floor creaked behind her. A puff of breath cracked the stillness.

Then something hard and blunt slammed against her skull.

Stars danced in front of her eyes, then the world faded away as she collapsed onto the floor and blacked out.

Chapter Seven

Someone had painted ugly words on the side of the new barns, then beaten the interior walls with a hammer and ripped apart the wooden slats on one of the stalls.

Brandon rubbed the back of his neck, irritated. It had to be teenagers, although why the hell would they drive so far from the city just to pull some stupid stunt like this? Then again, he and Johnny and Carter had been hellions, had vandalized a few places themselves, and had skirted juvenile detention more than once.

It was one reason he'd decided to help out at the Bucking Bronc Lodge.

Night had set in and lightning cracked the tops of the oaks and mesquite trees as he left two of his hands to clean up the mess. The scent of impending rain filled the air, a hazy fog settling over the dismal gray sky. Deciding Kim and Lucy had probably finished grooming Spots, he drove straight to the house.

As he climbed out, he scanned the yard for Lucy, but didn't see her. He did notice a pair of live oaks that would make a good spot for the fort he'd promised. He could built a platform between the trees, then make a rope ladder on one side, add a tire swing.... Maybe they would even add a second level....

His head was spinning with ideas as he kicked dirt from his boots and entered the house. The scent of spaghetti sauce filled the air, making his stomach grumble, and he paused to dip a finger in and taste it.

Damn, Kim could cook.

Of course she'd had to. Her old man sure as hell hadn't made them any meals, and they'd lost their mother when they were young. Kim had taken care of her bastard father and Johnny and never complained. Now she'd earned a counseling degree to help other troubled boys.

He'd liked her as a kid. He'd loved her as a teenager.

And he admired the hell out of her now.

Then he spotted Lucy's drawing on the kitchen table, a picture of him and her holding hands in a field of daisies beside her beloved Spots.

Emotions crowded his chest, and for a moment, his lungs tightened as he imagined working on the ranch all day, then coming home to dinner with Kim and Lucy. They would both be waiting with a smile and a hug....

But the house was quiet. Where were they?

Suddenly the timing of the vandalism made the hairs on his nape stand on end, and he strode through the house calling their names. "Kim? Lucy?"

The downstairs proved empty, so he raced up the steps two at a time. No one upstairs either. He told himself not to panic. They'd probably just taken a walk. Or maybe they'd gone to play with the kittens.

He jogged down the steps, then toward the barn, wanting them back inside the house before the storm. The wind intensified, swirling leaves and twigs across the path. The barn door squeaked as he hastily opened it and scanned the interior. Spots was tucked in his stall, already groomed and fed. Fatherly pride filled him. Lucy was an animal lover just like her mom.

Clouds rumbled as he vaulted back outside, then passed the riding pens to the storage barn.

But a streak of lighting illuminated Lucy's stuffed lamb. It was on the ground outside the side door.

His instincts roared to alert. Lucy wouldn't have left the lamb in the dirt....

Suddenly unable to breathe, he picked it up then hurried inside. The barn was pitch dark, making him more antsy, and he flipped the light switch, but it made a popping sound instead of lighting up. His nerves spiking, he grabbed a flashlight from the tack room and flicked it on, waving it across the barn between the empty stalls.

"Kim? Lucy? Are you in here?" He checked the first three stalls, adrenaline flooding him. "Kim? Lucy?"

The kittens meowed, and he peered in the last stall to the right and saw the mama cat curled in the box. But Lucy wasn't inside.

Outside the wind picked up, hurling a limb against the side of the barn, and thunder clapped, shaking the roof. Then a low moan echoed somewhere nearby.

He swung around, searching for the sound. The stall across from him.

He shoved through the stall door and froze.

Kim was lying in the shavings, deathly pale, blood seeping from a gash on her head.

KIM MOANED and tried to lift her head, but a throbbing pain knifed through her temple. She blinked against the darkness, and the world spun around her. Bile rose to her throat, and she sucked in a sharp breath to stem the nausea.

"Kim, honey, it's Brandon. What happened?" She felt his hands gently lifting her hair away from her crown, then heard a low curse. "Kim, talk to me. Where's Lucy?"

Slowly his words sank through the fog around her aching head, and a memory flashed back. She and Lucy...in the barn...looking for the kittens...the door slamming shut. Then pain...

Oh, God...

"Kim?" Brandon cradled her face between his hands.

Kim blinked, then looked into his eyes, willing the world to stay upright. "Lucy?"

Brandon's face blurred in front of her. "Where is she, Kim?"

Alarm streaked through her. "Here with me...but I passed out. Maybe she went to the house to get help...."

"No, she's not at the house, Kim. Someone hit you over the head."

Reality strangled her. "Lucy...where is she?" Frantic to find her daughter, she tried to stand, but a dizzy spell assaulted her and she swayed. "Brandon, we have to find her!"

"Let me call a medic and then we'll search—"

"No." Kim dug her nails into his arms for support and pushed to her feet, tears blurring her vision. "We have to look now. If someone has her, they could be getting away."

Panic streaked Brandon's face. "She wasn't in the horse barn or the house." Brandon's tone dropped a decibel as he lifted the lamb to her. "But I found this outside in the dirt."

A wave of cold terror washed over her as Brandon helped her outside.

"Lucy!" Kim cried. "Lucy, honey, where are you?"

"Lucy, answer me. It's Daddy!" Brandon shined the flashlight across the path leading into the wooded area behind the barn.

"Footprints," Brandon said as the light beam caught tracks in the dirt.

Kim followed the track marks to some scrub brush and noticed a rag beneath it. She untangled it, then sniffed the cloth, nausea slamming into her again. "Oh, my God, Brandon, he drugged Lucy."

Brandon snatched the cloth and took a sniff. "Dammit, it's chloroform."

Kim's legs buckled as the implication sank in. The person who'd attacked her had kidnapped her daughter.

Brandon's head reeled. Someone had stolen Lucy.

But why? And who? Carter?

Would he really chloroform a child, especially if he thought she was his?

He curved an arm around Kim's waist to support her. "Come on. You're going to the house and call the sheriff while I phone my foreman to organize a search party."

"But I want to go with you," Kim said.

"No." Brandon forced his voice to remain steady even though terror filled his throat. "If someone did kidnap her, they might call the house."

Pain made Kim's eyes look dazed, but she must have recognized his logic because she nodded. Then she leaned against him as they hurried toward the house. He helped her inside, then raced through the rooms again to make sure it was empty.

When he returned, Kim was holding a damp cloth to her head. Brandon grabbed an ice pack from the freezer, then examined Kim's injury. "Tell the sheriff to send some medics. You might need stitches or to go to the hospital."

"I'm fine," Kim said. "I just want to find Lucy."

"So do I," Brandon said. "But do it anyway. You suffered a blow to the head, Kim. We can't take chances. Lucy's going to need you."

And dammit, he needed her, too. He wanted to stay here now and comfort her. Apologize for shutting her out of his life years ago. For hurting her and not being there for Lucy.

But he didn't have time. Every second that passed meant the kidnapper might be getting farther and farther away with his daughter.

He shoved the phone at her, and her eyes looked tormented as she punched in the sheriff's number. Brandon retrieved one of his rifles from the locked gun case and left it beside her, then grabbed his pistol and phoned his ranch foreman as he jogged to the truck. "Walt, this is Brandon. Someone attacked Kim and kidnapped Lucy. I need you to call the other hands and organize a search party."

"Any idea who took her?" Walt asked.

He started to explain about Carter, but there wasn't time. "No. But arm yourself in case he has a weapon." Brandon hesitated. "And tell the guys to be careful. This is my daughter. I don't want her harmed."

"Got it."

Brandon flipped on the engine and pressed the gas; then he and Walt discussed dividing the ranch into quadrants for searching purposes. The storm clouds rumbled, growing darker and more ominous as he drove around to check each barn and stable in case the kidnapper had hidden out before trying to leave the ranch.

He scanned the dirt roads leading through the property, hunting for signs of another vehicle or a stray horse the kidnapper could have used to make his escape, searching for any clue as to how he had come in and left, but the storm clouds unleashed a torrent of rain that quickly washed away any tracks and made visibility difficult.

Sweat streamed down his neck. He tried to think logically.

Had the vandalism been an attempt to lure him away from Kim and provide an opportunity for the kidnapper to snatch Lucy?

More questions nagged at him. He'd been gone at least a couple of hours. How long had Kim been unconscious?

If the kidnapper had escaped on horseback, were they out in this storm? Had he parked a car nearby and already left the ranch?

He checked his cell phone, hoping, praying it would ring. That one of his ranch hands would uncover a lead.

That his little girl was safe...

That Carter was the one who'd abducted her.

At least if Carter believed Lucy was his daughter, he wouldn't hurt her.

But if a stranger had abducted her, his little girl could be in serious danger....

KIM STARED AT THE CLOCK as she waited on the sheriff to arrive, counting the minutes since Brandon had left. Where was he?

Dear God, please let him find Lucy.... Let her be safe and let him bring her back to me....

Too nervous to sit still but too dizzy to pace, she picked up the phone to call Johnny. But she remembered Brandon's comment about a ransom call, so she hung up, then grabbed her cell phone to use instead. Rain slashed the windows and roof, thunder roaring as she called her brother. What if Lucy was out in this storm? Her poor baby...

The phone jangled once, twice, three times, and she fidgeted, afraid he wasn't home, but he finally answered.

"Kim?"

"Johnny," Kim said breathlessly. "Someone kidnapped Lucy."

"What?" His raspy breath rattled over the line. "What do you mean, someone kidnapped her?"

Kim swallowed tears. "Lucy and I went to the barn to play with the kittens while Brandon checked on some vandalism, then someone hit me over the head, and knocked me out....." Her voice broke. "When I came to, she was gone."

"Dammit. Where's Brandon?" Johnny asked sharply.

"He called the ranch hands and they're searching the property." Kim clutched the lamb to her heart, rocking it back and forth as she would a child. "Johnny, do you think Carter did this?"

"I don't know," Johnny said gruffly. "He's desperate, but why would he hurt you and then take Lucy? Why not just confront you, talk to you both?"

Kim massaged her temple. "That's what I was thinking. He knows the police are after him."

"That's right. And adding kidnapping charges would only make things worse. Plus having Lucy would make it more difficult for him to hide out."

Cold fear crawled through Kim. "Unless he wants

to use her as a shield. Or to blackmail me into giving him money."

Johnny cursed. "That doesn't sound like Carter. I've offered to help him financially several times over the past five years, and he's practically thrown the offer back in my face."

A knock sounded at the door, and Kim jumped up and hurried toward it. "I think the sheriff is here now."

"Good. Fill him in, and if Carter calls demanding a ransom, let me know. I'll pay whatever he asks for Lucy's return."

"Thanks, Johnny. I knew I could count on you."

A heartbeat passed. "You can count on Brandon, too."

Words died in Kim's throat. She'd once believed that with all her heart. But now?

She didn't want to debate the issue with her brother. "Johnny, what if Carter didn't abduct Lucy?"

"Then we'll call in the feds, pay the ransom, do whatever we have to do." His voice wavered slightly. "But we will get Lucy back, Kim. Then Brandon and I will kill the SOB who snatched her."

Johnny's vehemence gave her strength, and she swiped at her tears, willing herself to be strong.

"Listen, Kim," Johnny said. "I'm going to phone that reporter who covered the rodeo. Maybe she can arrange some press for you and Brandon to spread the word about Lucy."

"Good. Tell her I'll do anything she wants if she'll help us."

She closed her phone, then sighed with relief at the sight of the sheriff's car in front of the house.

Kim threw the door open and waved him and his

deputy in. They shook rain from their hats and wiped their feet on the rug as they entered.

Sheriff McRae gestured to his sidekick, a younger, thin man in uniform, with short brown hair.

"This is Deputy Pikes."

The deputy nodded in greeting. "Ma'am, a paramedic team is on their way."

The sheriff gestured toward her blood-tinged hair. "You look like you need to sit down."

"My head will heal," Kim said, brushing off his concern. "But my daughter is missing and we have to find her."

Sheriff McRae removed a small notepad from his pocket. "Please, sit down. Then tell me exactly what happened."

Resigned, Kim collapsed on the couch while the sheriff claimed the club chair opposite her.

Her adrenaline surge was waning so she twined her fingers together.

"Did you see who attacked you?" the sheriff asked.

Kim shook her head. "No. He hit me from behind. And when I came to, Lucy was gone."

"You think this may be related to the break-in at the Bucking Bronc Lodge?" Sheriff McRae asked.

Kim shrugged. "It seems too coincidental not to be." She explained about the hit-and-run driver. "We weren't sure if that was connected. I thought maybe it was a drunk driver, but now I can't help but wonder."

The sheriff's scowl deepened the lines around his eyes. "It does sound suspicious. What kind of vehicle was it?"

"Some kind of truck," Kim said. "We didn't get a good look, though."

"How about the color?

"It was too dark and it happened so quickly," Kim said. "Then he flew on past."

"So you're still thinking that your buddy Carter might have broken in at the BBL, then followed you here and struck you to take your daughter?"

Kim nodded, then gestured toward the cloth they'd found on the ground. "We found that rag and Lucy's stuffed lamb near some scrub brush outside the barn. There were track marks across the dirt as if the kidnapper dragged her into the woods."

Sheriff McRae sniffed the rag. "You're right. Seems suspicious. But with this rain, I doubt we'll find more evidence tonight."

The deputy removed his cell phone from the clip at his belt. "I'll issue an Amber alert."

Sheriff McRae worked his mouth from side to side. "Kim, if you have a photograph we can air on the news and send to all the pertinent databases and law enforcement agencies, that would help." He turned to his deputy. "Also, Pikes, alert authorities that she might be traveling with an escaped felon."

Kim rushed to her purse and removed a picture of Lucy from her wallet, tears pulsing behind her eyes as she looked at her daughter smiling in the photograph. "This was taken on her last birthday," she said. "She's four."

Sheriff McRae studied the picture; then he handed it to the deputy. "She's a cutie." Sympathy softened his eyes as he met her gaze. "We'll do everything we can to find her, ma'am."

A siren wailed outside, lights twirling through the window sheers.

Deputy Pikes rushed to the front door to greet the paramedics, and Kim clenched her hands together, mentally reviewing the last few days in her mind. The attack at the Bucking Bronc, the hit-and-run, now another attack on her, and Lucy missing...

Why had someone targeted her and her daughter?

FRUSTRATION AND WORRY knotted every muscle in Brandon's body as he headed back to check on Kim. He and his hands had driven the property several times and searched every place he could think of, even an old abandoned mine on the far end of his land.

His gut told him that Lucy's kidnapper had left The Woodstock Wagoneer.

He checked his watch, then his phone, but Kim hadn't called. Not a good sign.

No ransom call might mean that Carter had Lucy and wanted to get to know her. Or it might mean that this kidnapping had nothing to do with Carter, which left him totally perplexed and terrified.

Because the other possibilities and scenarios were too horrible to imagine.

Lucy in the hands of a child molester or madman. Lucy being carted off to be sold like that child-kidnapping ring he'd heard about in Miami.

Lucy being abused or hurt....

No, he couldn't allow his mind to travel to those dark places. He had to remain strong and positive for Kim's sake.

And he had to find his daughter and make up for all the years they'd missed together.

He parked in front of the house and saw the ambulance and sheriff's car. Good God, this was a nightmare. Kim had been attacked twice.

And now Lucy was gone. He'd sworn he'd be a better man than his sorry-assed father.

But so far he'd failed miserably.

He would make this right, though.

Mentally he ticked through the past few days. If the kidnapper was the same person who'd broken in at the BBL, had he been watching them ever since?

It was possible.

He hadn't left Kim's or Lucy's sides since they'd arrived.

Until tonight.

His gut clenched.

The kidnapper had been waiting on him to leave Kim and Lucy alone, unprotected.

And the vandalism had given him his opening....

Dammit, he'd fallen right into the kidnapper's trap.

Chapter Eight

Brandon saw the strain on Kim's face as he entered the house. The medics were examining her so he went straight to the sheriff and deputy.

"Did you find anything?" Sheriff McRae asked.

"No." Brandon jammed his hands in his pockets to keep from pounding the walls. "Some of my men are still searching. The bastard probably left the ranch, but Kim's brother, Johnny, is bringing his chopper and we're going back out to search some more." He glanced at the phone. "No ransom call?"

The sheriff shook his head. "We issued an Amber alert and set up a tip line. And my deputy faxed her picture nationwide and to NCMEC, the National Center for Missing and Exploited Children."

Brandon nodded, his body riddled with tension. He had to do more. Should be doing more.

"Miss Long filled us in on the hit-and-run, and the possibility that Flagstone might have followed you here." The sheriff tapped his pad with his pen. Brandon explained his theory about the vandalism being a diversion. "Could be," Sheriff McRae said. "Can you think of any place Carter might go or take Lucy?"

Brandon sighed and scrubbed his hand over his face,

grateful for the questions. He was too damn upset to think straight.

"He might go to his old man's ranch," he said. "His dad died a few weeks ago, but he owned a spread on the north side of San Antonio. It's probably deserted."

The sheriff made a sound in his throat. "Sounds like a logical place to hide."

Brandon nodded, then cited the address. But anxiety clawed at him. The trouble was, it would be the natural place for the cops to look. So where else would Carter go?

He sure as hell didn't have any friends that Brandon knew of. Other than him and Johnny. And Carter had written them off long ago.

Unless he'd made friends in prison. The thought made his blood turn to ice.

If one of them had Lucy, there was no telling what he might do to her....

He inhaled sharply, desperate to think logically.

Even if Carter wasn't involved, if his friends were aware of his relationship with Johnny and Brandon, or if Carter had spouted off about Lucy and been mad at Kim for not bringing her to see him, maybe one of them had decided to kidnap her and use her to pay their way out of town. Both he and Johnny's success stories had been featured in the papers. And the rodeo at the Bucking Bronc Lodge had upped publicity for the ranch and for them as investors, painting them as among the wealthiest men in Texas.

"We're operating on the assumption that your buddy Carter abducted your daughter," Sheriff McRae said. "But what if he didn't? Do you or the lady have any other enemies?"

Brandon chewed the possibility over in his head as he explained his theory about the publicity.

"You're right," McRae said. "Being two of the most wealthy ranchers in Texas can draw random crazies."

Brandon's stomach roiled. All this time he'd wanted money and recognition. Now it might have endangered his child.

"I asked Miss Long about former lovers or ex-boyfriends who might hold a grudge against her." The sheriff folded his arms. "But she couldn't think of anyone. How about you? Other than Carter Flagstone, is there anyone you know personally who'd want to target you, Mr. Woodstock? A disgruntled employee? A business associate you've crossed? An ex-lover or wife?"

"Let me think about that." Brandon's anxiety mounted as he contemplated the enemies he might have made. Sure, he'd stepped on a few toes along the way to success. Bought up some land out from under a couple of guys who planned to bring in mining or some other operation that wouldn't sit well beside his ranch.

But they wouldn't kidnap Lucy in retaliation. Would they?

No…the fact that he had a child wasn't public knowledge.

And Marty didn't need the money. She had no idea Lucy was his either. Hell, he hadn't known until a few days ago.

"Think about it some more and make a list," the sheriff said. "Have Miss Long's brother do the same. Bigwig like Johnny Long is a perfect target for a kidnapper."

Brandon nodded. He'd pick his brain for names and

fax them to the sheriff ASAP. He just hoped they found Lucy tonight or that Carter called.

He didn't want to contemplate the other possibilities. Or that they might not see Lucy again at all.

KIM SUFFERED THROUGH the paramedics' exam but refused to go to the hospital, so she signed the necessary forms and sent the ambulance packing. She had to be near the house in case the kidnapper called.

It had to be Carter. It had to be....

Although the sheriff's questions about Brandon's enemies raised doubts. Had his success garnered a stalker or crazy person who'd seen the latest publicity on him, learned Lucy was his child, and targeted them?

Her poor little girl...was she alive? Safe?

A knock sounded at the door, and she tensed and met Brandon's gaze. The sheriff gestured to let him handle it, then went to see who was outside.

Brandon inched closer to her, his dark gaze so tormented that she was tempted to reach out and console him.

"Are you okay?" he asked gruffly.

She stiffened, forcing herself not to lean on him. How could she answer that question? Physically she would survive. But without her daughter...

"Kim?" he said gruffly.

"I can't believe this is happening. I almost lost Lucy once. I can't lose her now."

His brows furrowed. "What do you mean, you almost lost her once?"

Voices interrupted, cutting off their conversation. She hadn't meant to reveal that detail about her past and didn't want to share the painful memory with Brandon.

A tall, attractive woman wearing a royal-blue suit

and heels strode toward her. "Hi, I'm June Warner. Johnny Long asked me to do an interview regarding his niece's kidnapping."

Brandon looked at Kim with questions in his eyes, and she nodded. "I talked to Johnny. He set it up."

"Good," Brandon said, then lowered his voice. "But if Carter sees an interview of us together, he'll know Lucy isn't his."

Kim rubbed her forehead. "I hadn't thought of that."

The vein in Brandon's neck throbbed. "Maybe you should do the interview alone," he suggested. "At this point, we don't know what frame of mind Carter is in. All we know is that he's desperate and has anger issues. We don't want to do anything to piss him off or jeopardize Lucy."

Perspiration beaded on her forehead. "You're right." Kim offered her hand in greeting as June approached. "I'm Kim, Johnny's sister."

"Right, I remember you from the Bucking Bronc Lodge," June said with a sympathetic smile. "Your brother explained that you think one of the prison escapees may have abducted your little girl." The woman waved a cameraman inside. "This is Robbie. He'll film the interview, then we'll get the clip on the air ASAP and run it until Lucy is found."

Kim wiped her clammy palms on the pants of her jeans, then shook his hand. "Thanks for coming."

June squeezed Kim's arm. "Hang in there, Kim," June said, then adopted her professional mode. "Now, first, I'll make the introduction to the story, give the sheriff a minute to fill in the details, then we'll turn the camera on you."

Nerves knotted Kim's stomach. "What should I say?"

"Just be yourself." June offered an encouraging smile. "At the end, we'll post the number for the police department and Lucy's photo, as well as the special tip line for people to call if they have any information regarding her disappearance. Sometimes family or friends of kidnappers are suspicious and will call in themselves when they realize their loved one has committed a crime."

"Carter doesn't have any family," Kim said.

Brandon pressed a hand to the small of her back. "We don't know for certain that Carter abducted Lucy, Kim. Maybe someone spotted him and Lucy, and we can track them down."

Kim nodded mutely, then ran a hand through her hair as the cameraman set up. She'd been through hell and back tonight and probably looked a fright, but she didn't care. They had to do everything they could to ensure Lucy's safe return.

"This is June Warner bringing you a breaking story. We're at the home of Brandon Woodstock, owner of the Woodstock Wagoneer. A guest and friend of his, Kim Long, sister of famous rodeo star Johnny Long, was assaulted on the Woodstock property tonight, and her attacker abducted her four-year-old daughter, Lucy."

She pushed the mic toward the sheriff. "Sheriff, can you tell us more on this terrible incident?"

"As Miss Weaver said, four-year-old Lucy Long was kidnapped tonight." Sheriff McRae widened his stance. "At this point we have reason to believe that Carter Flagstone, one of the escapees from the state penitentiary who was serving a life sentence for murder, may have kidnapped her." He flashed a picture of Carter. "If you see this man or this little girl, please contact the local police or the number on your screen."

The reporter smiled, then motioned to Kim to step forward. Kim silently prayed for courage as she faced the camera.

"Miss Long," June said. "Would you like to say a few words?"

Kim took a deep breath before speaking. "My name is Kim Long," she said in a shaky voice. "My little girl Lucy is only four years old, just an innocent little girl. She's missing, and I...love her and...want her back." She had to pause to gather her composure. "I don't know who you are or why you took her. But if it's you, Carter, or someone else, please, please, I beg you, just don't hurt her. I'll do anything you say, pay your ransom, meet your demands, just keep her safe and send her back home where she belongs."

Her tears spilled over and she swiped at them with trembling fingers.

June squeezed her elbow, then reclaimed the mic. "As you can see, Miss Long is devastated over tonight's events, and desperately needs help finding her young daughter. Once again, if you have any information regarding the abduction or Carter Flagstone's whereabouts, please contact the police."

A numbness settled over Kim as the reporter and cameraman packed up and left.

The Sheriff turned to Brandon. "The FBI is going to put a trace on your phone and hook your cells up to the landline in case you need to leave the house. Call me if you hear anything. And send me that list of anyone suspicious from your past."

Brandon shook his hand. "I will. Thanks, Sheriff."

Sheriff McRae gave her another sympathetic look; then he and his deputy walked out the door. Outside the rain was still pounding, lightning streaked the sky and thunder rumbled in the ominous silence.

Exhausted and overwrought with emotions, Kim swayed on her feet. Brandon's eyes raked over her, his dark look feral.

She should have taken better care of Lucy. Was he thinking that, too?

Tears clogged her throat, and she started toward the stairs, but Brandon caught her and drew her into his arms. She collapsed against him, needing his strength and courage, needing his reassurance that their little girl would come home alive.

Without Lucy, her life would mean nothing.

BRANDON CRADLED KIM in his arms and rubbed her back to soothe her. She had suffered a terrible ordeal tonight, and he was amazed she hadn't collapsed before.

"Let me walk you upstairs. You have a head injury, Kim. You need to rest."

She shook her head against his chest. Her tears soaked his shirt, but he didn't care. He desperately wanted to assuage her pain.

Self-recriminations screamed through his head. If he hadn't gone to check on that vandalism, he would have been here, able to protect them. Which raised suspicions again that the vandalism had been a ploy to separate them.

"I can't rest," Kim said in a strangled voice. "Not until we find Lucy."

"Then sit down and let me fix you a drink."

Kim nodded and he guided her to the sofa. "Wine or tea?" Brandon asked.

"Just water." Kim picked up the stuffed lamb and hugged it to her as if it were a baby.

He went to the bar and poured her a glass of water and himself a brown whiskey, then returned to the couch and sat down beside her.

"I should have stayed in the house with Lucy," Kim said, her hand shaking as she cradled the glass with her palms. "It was dark and I should have waited for you to return, but Lucy wanted to see the kitties and I thought we were safe here."

So had he. "It's not your fault, Kim. I shouldn't have left you alone."

Her tortured gaze met his, tears brimming on her lashes. "We can't lose her, Brandon. I...can't...even think about life without Lucy."

His throat tightened. "We won't, Kim. I promise I'll bring her back to you if it's the last thing I ever do."

Her gaze fell to the glass of water, and she stared into it as if it might hold answers. Her earlier comment echoed in his head.

"What did you mean when you said that you almost lost Lucy once? Did someone try to kidnap her before?"

"No..." Kim sipped the water and set the glass on the coffee table. She looked weary, blood still dotting her hair.

He massaged the base of her neck hoping to help alleviate the tension knotting her shoulders. "Then what did you mean?"

Kim tucked an errant strand of hair behind one ear. "Early in the pregnancy, I almost had a miscarriage."

Brandon gritted his teeth. "What caused it?"

Kim released a labored sigh. "Who knows? Tension, stress...there are a million reasons women miscarry."

His mind registered the obvious. "But you were under enormous stress because you were alone."

Kim traced a bead of water from the glass. "That's not what I meant, Brandon."

"But it's true." He tossed down his drink, grateful for the slow burn of alcohol. Although nothing could ease his guilt. "What happened then?"

"The doctors ordered me on bed rest, and I thought the worst was over. But toward the end of the third trimester, I developed preeclampsia."

"Preeclampsia?"

The ice in the glass clinked as Kim set it down on the coffee table. "I developed high blood pressure. It causes gestational hypertension."

Brandon sensed he wasn't going to like the rest of the story, but he had to know anyway. "Go on."

Kim shook her head. "It's not important now, Brandon. That was four years ago."

"It is important," Brandon said. "Tell me the truth, Kim. Everything."

Kim's voice warbled. "Lucy and I both almost died during the birth."

And while she'd been suffering and nearly died giving birth to their little girl, what had he been doing?

Signing a deal with the devil to make enough money to bring his little sister home and save her.

But he'd lost her. And his child and the only woman he'd ever loved had nearly died as a result.

And now Lucy was gone...

What if he never got her back?

Kim closed her eyes to block out the horrific memories of that traumatic night. She'd needed Brandon so badly that she'd almost caved and begged Johnny to call him.

"I should have been there," Brandon said. "You should have called."

Anger rolled through her, and she stood and jammed her hands on her hips. "I should have called? Why, Brandon? So you could remind me that you didn't love me?"

"Kim—"

She slashed her hand through the air, cutting him off. "In fact, the night I went to the hospital, I had just seen another story about you and Marty at some charity function on the news. Your wife looked like a million dollars in a long gown and diamonds." All her pent-up emotions bubbled over. "You were beaming with joy. You had a gorgeous bride by your side, were glowing in the light of the social world that promised you all your dreams."

She poked him in the chest.

"So what was I supposed to do?" Her voice shook with fury. "Ask you to leave the woman you loved to visit your ex-girlfriend and illegitimate child? Beg you to sit with me and hold my hand for the night and pretend you cared?"

Brandon's face turned ashen, but Kim couldn't hold back the words. They spilled over.

"I'm sorry, Kim," Brandon said in a deep, anguished voice. "I... You have no idea how sorry I am."

"I didn't want your pity then," Kim shouted. "And I don't want it now."

He closed her fingers around his arm. "It's not pity, dammit. And it wouldn't have been back then."

"Then what would it have been, Brandon? Guilt?" A sarcastic laugh escaped her. "For God's sake, you would have thought I was trying to trap you."

A smoky hue settled over his eyes. A hue she used to think was sensual. Hunger.

Love.

But she'd been a fool.

"Kim...things were complicated—"

"No, they were simple," Kim said. "You didn't love me, you loved her."

She jerked away and went to the window and looked out, willing someone to bring her daughter back. Willing the phone to ring.

A million emotions warred inside her. Kim wanted to believe he would have cared, but his actions had proved differently. Besides, she couldn't deal with her feelings toward him now. Not when she was so raw from the attack.

Not when she was so terrified that she might never see Lucy again.

"Like I said earlier," she said between clenched teeth, "it doesn't matter about the past. All that matters is finding our daughter."

Pain darkened his eyes, but Kim couldn't allow herself to have empathy for him. So she grabbed her cell phone and ran upstairs. She needed to be alone. To pray for Lucy. To pray for herself, too.

He could be a father to Lucy.

But she would never trust him with her heart again.

Chapter Nine

Brandon had almost confessed the truth.

But how could he admit that he'd made the worst mistake of his life by marrying Marty when Kim was so terrified about losing Lucy?

Besides, after the way he'd hurt her, he had no right to expect her forgiveness.

Dammit, he'd ruined his chances of ever earning her trust or love.

His body taut, he strode outside on the front porch and inhaled the night air. The rain had slowed to a drizzle, the ranch muddied by the hazy fog of gray clouds. Still, the rolling pastures and hills were beautiful to the eyes. This ranch and his house—they had consumed his dreams for years.

He'd built the porch and the porch swing himself, modeling it after that magazine picture Kim had taped on the wall of her dilapidated house when she was fifteen. As he'd pounded the nails and hung the swing, he'd remembered the times they'd talked and laughed and dreamed together. Their first kiss and the first time they'd made love and the promises he'd made and broken.

He and Marty had never dreamed together. She'd

laughed at his ideas of a quiet ranch life, had scoffed at the idea of working on a ranch and dirtying her hands. She'd wanted a fancy mansion in the city, a maid and a cook, and to travel and hobnob with the wealthy socialites.

All he'd wanted was a home to bring his sister to, to rescue her from that godforsaken hole-in-the-wall home, where he suspected the residents weren't always treated well. It had been nothing he could prove, but the idea of someone abusing or taking advantage of Joanie had killed him.

Marty had thought she could change him. That he'd buy his land and let someone else handle the day-to-day business of ranching while he flitted around the world with her. She'd expected him to hire someone to care for Joanie, and had even balked when he'd wanted to set up a trust fund in her name and start a charity foundation to raise money for research for her disorder.

But he'd insisted on the charity. And he hadn't relented to her demands to not work on his own spread either. By god, he was a hands-on rancher, a man who breathed and lived for the land and his ranch, a man who was more comfortable in the saddle than on a jet. A man who put family first, not a social calendar. He had no desire to join her elitist world. And she'd had no desire to ride, much less live out in the wilderness.

Even worse, she'd been embarrassed when he'd wanted to bring Joanie home for Christmas.

They had been so different that they'd been doomed from the start. And after just a few years, their marriage was over.

A knock sounded at the door, and he rushed to answer it. Johnny stood there, anxious and sweating. "The chopper is gassed up. How's Kim?"

"She's upstairs," Brandon said. "Let's go."

Brandon grabbed his night binoculars, and they hurried to the chopper. He scanned the property as Johnny lifted off.

"I can't believe this is happening," Johnny said. "First Carter escapes. Now Lucy goes missing."

"He has to have her," Brandon said.

Johnny gestured toward the north quadrant, where the land was more deserted, and Brandon studied it but saw no movement. "At least if he does, we know she's not in danger."

Johnny sighed. "Listen, man, you'd better hang in there with Kim right now. She needs you."

Brandon gritted his teeth. "I don't need a lecture from you, Johnny. Lucy is my little girl. I would have been there for her before if I'd known about her."

"Would you have?"

Johnny's question cut him to the bone. "I realize we had our differences, Johnny, but you know me better than that."

"I thought I did, but then you broke Kim's heart."

So Johnny still harbored resentment against him for that. After what Kim had told him tonight about nearly dying and losing Lucy, how could he blame him? He should have been beside Kim during the pregnancy; he should have been taking care of her instead of Johnny.

"I deserve that," Brandon said. "I messed up. But I..." *I love Kim.* No, he couldn't confess his feelings. He had to redeem himself first. "I promise to take care of her now and bring Lucy home."

A long, tense beat passed; then Johnny cleared his throat. "Good. Just don't hurt her again, Brandon. Kim's been through a lot the last four years. She deserves some happiness. Someone who really loves her and won't abandon her."

Like you did years ago.

The brutal truth echoed over and over in Brandon's head as they searched. Twice, Brandon thought he might have spotted a truck or car, then realized it was two of his men still searching as he'd asked.

Finally after hours of nothing, he and Johnny had to call it a night. Rational thoughts told him that the kidnapper wouldn't hide out on his own property with Lucy anyway.

So where had he taken her?

Johnny set the chopper down and made Brandon swear to call him the minute he heard anything.

"I'm going to look over my employee files for anything suspicious," Brandon said. "And start putting together some cash in case we get a ransom call."

"I'll do the same."

The house was quiet as Brandon entered, and he made a pot of coffee and strode to his office. He accessed his financials to review, then emailed his accountant asking him to liquidate some assets and put together some cash.

He'd give up everything he had, his money, his ranch, his business, whatever the bastard wanted, just to hold his little girl in his arms again.

KIM COULDN'T SLEEP so she slipped into Lucy's room and combed through the toys she'd brought for her daughter. Lucy's doll Johnny had given her last year for her birthday, the coloring books and crayons, her picture books, and the Lambie. Knowing it was morose but unable to help herself, she went to the closet and stared at Lucy's clothes.

The colorful T-shirts and tiny jeans and her extra pair of sneakers with the purple ties. The ribbons she liked to wear in her hair. The pair of shorts with the ruffled pockets and matching shirt.

The little pink and white polka-dotted dress she'd bought for her last Easter. The only dress Kim had brought because she hadn't expected them to stay more than a day or two.

Fighting more tears, she clutched Lambie to her and sank onto the bed, then picked up Lucy's pillow and inhaled her sweet little-girl scent and the strawberry shampoo she loved.

Lucy's yellow pj's with the bunnies on them lay on the floor where Lucy had discarded them, and her chest heaved on a sob. Where was her daughter? Was the kidnapper treating her with care? Where would Lucy sleep tonight?

Sheer terror threatened to overpower her, but she forced images of what Lucy might be enduring to the back of her mind. If Carter had her, he would keep her safe. She had to believe that. She couldn't think any other way.

It had to be Carter, not some other maniac.

Her head began to throb again, and she curled on the bed. She wouldn't go to sleep. But she had to stop the incessant pounding in her head so she closed her eyes. Fatigue finally overcame her though, and she dozed into a fitful sleep.

Hours later, Kim jerked awake, a weak thread of light breaking through the darkness. The rain had ended sometime during the night.

But her nightmare was still real.

Suddenly anxious to see if Brandon might have heard news, she jumped out of bed, then ran to the bathroom and washed her face. A quick look in the mirror revealed bags under her eyes and disheveled hair with blood still staining the ends. She ran a brush through it, then headed downstairs. Her pulse was racing with worry, and she silently prayed that Carter had brought Lucy back and she'd be waiting in the kitchen with Brandon....

She picked up her pace, then rounded the corner into the kitchen. A fresh pot of coffee sat on the counter, but no one was there. Then Brandon's voice echoed from the master suite.

She hadn't been inside his room yet, hadn't wanted to see where he had shared a bed with another woman, but she had to forget her pride. Still, she paused at his doorway, her pulse pounding at his words.

"Yes, just have the cash ready," Brandon said. "I don't care how much he wants. I'll give him the whole damn ranch in exchange for Lucy."

Kim's heart squeezed at the intensity in Brandon's voice. He might not love Kim, but his feelings for Lucy were obvious. He'd go to the extreme to save her, just as he had his little sister.

She knocked softly, then stepped into the doorway. Brandon was pacing, his movements jerky, his jaw set stubbornly. A pair of well-worn jeans hung low on his lean hips, his broad chest shirtless, muscles bunching in his arms as he clenched the phone. He looked tired and worried, and his hair was sticking up as if he'd run his hands through it a dozen times.

She gave a quick glance at the room and was surprised to see it was more masculine than feminine. A giant oak sleigh bed, covered in a dark blue quilt, dominated the space. A fireplace hugged one corner and

French doors led outside to the side porch, offering a breathtaking view of the hills and lush pastures.

He pivoted as if he sensed she was there; then his gaze locked with hers. His eyes glittered with turmoil and other emotions she couldn't define. But his hard, lean, muscular body robbed her breath and vaulted her back to a time when she would have run into his arms without a second's hesitation.

God...so much had changed.

Then he spoke into the phone. "Yes, I'll stay in touch." When he disconnected the call, he grabbed a denim shirt from the bed and yanked it on, although he didn't button it right away.

"Did you receive a ransom call?" Kim asked.

Frustration flattened his mouth into a thin line. "I haven't heard a damn thing."

Kim sagged with disappointment. "But you were getting money together—"

"I wanted to be prepared," Brandon said. "To have cash available just in case."

Kim nodded in understanding although she didn't understand any of this. "Have you talked to the sheriff? Did they search Carter's father's place?"

Brandon sighed and began buttoning his shirt. "I called him about a half hour ago. He sent some men over, but he said it didn't look like anyone had been at the ranch in months."

Kim threw up her hands. "Where else would Carter go?"

"I don't know." Brandon scrubbed his hand over his chin, where beard stubble had started to grow. "Johnny and I both thought he would show up at his place or here. And he could have vandalized the barn to draw me away from you so he could snatch Lucy."

Kim wrung her hands together as panic bubbled inside her. "You don't think he'd try to cross the border, do you?"

Brandon rubbed her arms. "If he does, the border patrol will stop him." His breath whooshed out. "Besides, I don't think Carter's escape is about leaving the country. After the rodeo Johnny hired a P.I. to investigate Carter's case. He claimed there was a woman who could alibi him. The P.I. was murdered right before Carter escaped, so Johnny thinks Carter is going to track her down and try to clear himself."

"But why carry Lucy if he's on a wild goose chase?" A shudder rippled through her as she envisioned Carter being caught, facing armed cops prepared to shoot him, with Lucy in the middle. "What if he uses Lucy as a shield or a hostage? What if the police find him and she gets hurt in the cross fire?"

Brandon cupped her face between his hands. "Stop it, Kim. We can't imagine the worst."

"How can I not?" Kim asked. "Lucy was stolen from me and she's been gone overnight—"

"Shh…" he whispered. "I promise you we'll find her."

Exhaustion and terror made her lash out. "Your promises don't mean anything to me anymore."

Brandon's face clouded. "I'm sorry, Kim…. I wish I could change the past, take back the way I treated you."

"But you can't," Kim said, her voice cracking.

Heat sizzled between them as he stared at her. All the hurt and blame and the raw ache that she had lived with for so long was still there.

But God help her, she still wanted him.

His breath whispered out, a pained sound that tore

at her. He was suffering. She knew that. He'd just discovered he had a child and now he'd lost her.

"Maybe not," he said gruffly. "But I swear on my sister's grave that I won't stop until Lucy is back with us."

Kim's throat thickened at the same time her heart yearned to believe him, to trust him again. His gaze met hers, pleading, tormented, hungry. The need and loneliness she'd felt the last four years swelled inside her, begging for the reprieve only Brandon could offer her.

He must have sensed her need because he angled his head and lowered his lips to hers. Kim tasted the heady combination of desire, potent masculinity and raw primal lust as his tongue teased her lips apart and he claimed her mouth with his.

She had wanted him for so long that she couldn't help herself.

She gave in to him and returned the kiss, then threaded her hands in his hair, silently begging for more.

BRANDON HAD CRAVED Kim for years.

Having her here now in his arms only reminded him what a fool he had been to leave her. He had never felt this intense passion and heat for Marty. He'd never wanted to tear off her clothes or bury himself inside her.

He had never wanted to marry her either.

Only he had and he'd ruined things with Kim.

But Kim moved against him, tunneling her fingers in his hair and drawing him closer, and her tongue danced with his in a mating ritual that heated his blood and made him crazy with desire. And he forgot about

Marty. All he could think about was that he was finally kissing Kim again.

He dropped one hand to her hip to pull her more snugly against him, and she made a small moaning sound that intensified his hunger.

His sex surged to life, aching and throbbing for her, and he stroked her hip, moving against her, then kissed and nibbled his way down her throat. Kim leaned into him with a sigh, then slipped one hand inside his shirt to rub his chest. His heartbeat picked up, beating so fast that he felt like he would explode. She had to feel it beneath her palm, feel the heat in his body, the need and desire that he'd denied himself, the need and desire that had never died.

Wanting her closer, aching to feel her bare skin against his fingers, to have her naked beside him, to plunge himself inside her and remind her how wonderful they were together both outside the bedroom and inside, he walked her backward toward the bed.

But the moment he lowered her onto the mattress, she stiffened and pushed him away. He froze, hurting, wanting her more than he could voice, and even more confused by the stark look of passion still blazing in her eyes.

"Kim?"

"We can't do this," she whispered. "Not here."

He gently brushed a strand of hair from her cheek. "But I just want to comfort you, I—"

"No." She stood, her expression haunted. "Not here, not in this bed where you slept with another woman."

Her voice quivered; then she raced past him without waiting for his response. He gritted his teeth as he heard the kitchen door slam, then forced himself to remain still and give her time. He had to be patient.

Besides, even if he did confess his love, she wouldn't believe him.

He had to prove it. Earn her trust and forgiveness.

Because if she couldn't forgive him, there was no way they could ever be a family.

And he didn't just want Lucy back.

Dammit. He wanted Kim.

KIM DESPERATELY NEEDED some air. She had almost lost herself and made love with Brandon.

But she could not give herself to him physically without offering him her heart and soul.

And that was too risky.

For all she knew, he might still love Marty. She didn't know the details of the divorce. He might be hoping for a reconciliation.

And then…where would that leave her? Out of his life again.

Except for Lucy.

How would Marty feel about their daughter?

Her chest heaved as she ran across the yard to the barn. Seeing Spots would make her feel closer to Lucy. Lucy loved the horse so much…. What if she didn't come home and never got to ride him again?

Tears pricked at her eyes again, but she blinked furiously to stem them as she hurried into the barn. Horses from the first two stalls neighed and whinnied, and she petted them briefly, then made her way to the paint.

Just as she reached Spots's stall, someone grabbed her from behind. Kim tried to scream, but a hard cold hand clamped over her mouth.

She kicked and tried to jab him with her elbow, but his grip tightened as he dragged her into the empty stall in the back.

Chapter Ten

Brandon had to go after Kim and straighten things out. In spite of their feelings for each other, they had to pull together and be strong to find their daughter.

She would bind them together forever.

He had just found her. He refused to lose her.

Even if he couldn't have Kim...

No. By god, he would have them both.

But he couldn't dwell on that now or pressure Kim. Time was of the essence.

His stomach knotted and he glanced out the kitchen window, alert, searching for Kim. Maybe he shouldn't have let her go outside alone.

A bad premonition suddenly tugged at his gut. If the kidnapper had been working with a partner and had intended to hurt Kim, he might still be close by.

And he might come back to finish the job.

He had to find her.

THE MAN'S ARM PRESSED against Kim's windpipe so tightly she gasped for air.

But adrenaline surged through her. She would not let this guy kill her. She had to fight.

She gritted her teeth, remembering the self-defense

lessons Johnny and Brandon had taught her, then brought her left foot up and kicked backward aiming for his knee. But her attacker was too fast and dodged the blow.

"Be still," the man growled. "I'm not going to hurt you. I just want to talk."

Kim froze, her mind racing. Was this some kind of ploy to trap her into relaxing? Then he'd kill her?

"Let me go," she whispered.

He jerked her tighter against him, and Kim felt his rock-hard chest against her back. He was a big man. Tall, muscular. And too damn strong for her. "Please… let me go."

He wrapped his leg around her, pinning her so tightly her arms throbbed. "Not until you stop fighting."

Kim closed her eyes, battling the urge to scream. She needed to use her head and convince him to tell her where he was holding Lucy. "All right." She forced herself to relax, praying she wasn't making a mistake. "Where's my daughter?"

He eased up on his grip but still held her in front of him. She struggled to turn around. She wanted to see his face.

"I don't have Lucy," he growled. Then his hands dropped to her arms, and he spun her around to face him.

The barn was dark, but a sliver of moonlight played off the man's chiseled face. A jagged scar slashed his left cheek, his wide jaw was bruised, his eyes cold pits of ice. He looked older and worn, hardened and mean.

But she recognized him anyway. "Carter?" Fury made her voice brittle. "Where is she, dammit?"

Suddenly the barn door screeched open, and she heard Brandon's voice. "Kim, are you in here?"

Carter whipped a gun from inside his jacket and grabbed her arm.

"Brandon!" Kim cried.

"You have to listen to me, Kim," Carter whispered.

Brandon's eyes widened as he halted in front of them. His look turned feral at the sight of Carter holding her hostage. "Dammit, Carter," Brandon said between clenched teeth. "You've gone too far now. Let her go."

A shudder rippled up Kim's spine as the men faced off like two bulls ready to gore one another. All the times they'd fought as boys and teenagers flashed in her mind. One minute they'd be friends, the next throwing fists and brawling like animals.

But they'd always patched things up.

Until the night she'd slept with Carter...

Carter waved the gun, his nails digging into Kim's arm. "Just stay there, Brandon. We have to talk."

"Talk?" Brandon snarled. "The only thing we have to talk about is Lucy. Where is she, Carter? What have you done with her?"

"I didn't kidnap Lucy," Carter snapped. "That's what I came here to tell you."

"Don't lie to me," Brandon said in a lethal tone. "If you want money, you've got it. Just give us back Lucy. That's all we want."

Carter released a string of curses. "Listen to me, Brandon. I told you, I didn't take Lucy. You're wasting time blaming me when you need to be looking somewhere else."

Kim's panicked gaze shot to Brandon's. Carter sounded sincere.

BUSINESS REPLY MAIL
FIRST-CLASS MAIL   PERMIT NO. 717   BUFFALO, NY

POSTAGE WILL BE PAID BY ADDRESSEE

THE READER SERVICE
PO BOX 1867
BUFFALO NY 14240-9952

NO POSTAGE
NECESSARY
IF MAILED
IN THE
UNITED STATES

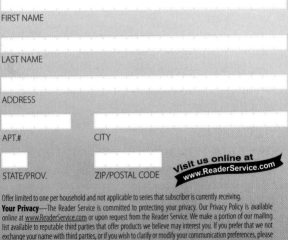

Brandon folded his arms across his massive chest. "Look, Carter, I know we had our differences. We fought. I didn't show up at your trial and give you an alibi—"

"This is not about us or our past," Carter said in a seething tone.

Then his face softened and he gave Kim an imploring look, reminding her of how gentle and loving he could be at times. Of the way he'd comforted her and held her the night she'd cried in his arms after Brandon had crushed her heart.

"I know I was angry the last time I saw you, Kim, but I swear on my little brother's grave that I did not kidnap Lucy. You knew me once. You know I would never harm a child."

The pain in Carter's tone made Kim's heart squeeze.

But on the heels of relief, panic and fear hit her. If Carter hadn't kidnapped Lucy, someone else had.

Which meant Lucy could be in terrible danger.

BRANDON DIDN'T KNOW what to believe. As a kid, he'd trusted Carter implicitly. As bullheaded teenagers, they'd fought and scrimmaged. But they had also formed a bond through those troubled years. A code that they'd lived by. They were blood brothers. They had each other's backs. *Always.*

Then Carter had slept with Kim.

"I know you're still bitter about me and Kim," Carter said. He suddenly released Kim, his look full of regret. "But you have to accept some blame, too, man. You left her. I just stepped in to comfort her."

"You mean you jumped in her bed the moment I left it," Brandon said.

Carter's scar reddened with his scowl. "That's not how it happened—"

"Stop it, you two!" Kim shouted. "Right now, Lucy is all that matters!"

Brandon knew Kim was right, but Carter had betrayed him.

Then again, you betrayed Kim first.

Kim folded her arms across her middle. "You really didn't kidnap Lucy?" Kim asked, her voice haunted.

Carter shook his head. "No, Kim. Why would you think it was me?"

"I thought you believed Lucy was yours. That you wanted to see her." Kim's lower lip quivered. "And I thought you hated me."

Disappointment streaked Carter's tortured eyes. "I did see that picture of you and Lucy at the rodeo. And for a minute, I hoped that she was mine." He rubbed at the scar on his forehead. "The past five years, you don't know what it's been like. I lost everything. My freedom. My friends. My chance at a future." He squeezed his eyes shut for a moment, then opened them, looking haunted. "And when I first saw Lucy, I thought maybe I had something out here to live for."

Brandon's heart twisted.

"But the moment I saw Lucy's green eyes, I knew she wasn't mine. She was Brandon's."

Brandon silently cursed. Only he hadn't figured it out because he'd been too wrapped up in the end of his sordid marriage.

Carter turned to Brandon. "I've had five long years in jail to think about what's important, man. Five years that I've missed building my own spread, having a family. You're a damn fool to have left Kim, and a bigger fool if you don't make up for hurting her."

Carter was right.

He did need to make it up to Kim. But first...Lucy.

"So if you didn't kidnap Lucy," Kim said, her voice breaking, "who did, and where is she?"

Carter's eyes filled with worry. "I have no idea. But I swear I had nothing to do with her disappearance."

Brandon's anger faded. "Then you risked your life by coming here, Carter. You know the state is crawling with cops looking for you."

Carter jammed the gun back inside his jacket. "Yeah, I saw that press report Kim did." He turned back to her with beseeching eyes. "But I had to come back. I couldn't let you believe that I abducted Lucy. And I didn't want the police wasting time looking for me for the crime when they needed to be investigating someone else."

So even after the terrible rift between the three of them, Carter had put his life on the line for them. Maybe it was time he returned the favor. "Carter, what's going on? Why did you break out?"

"I didn't plan to break out," Carter said. "But the day before the escape, I found out the P.I. Johnny hired was murdered. When the bus crashed, and the other two guys offered me the key, I took it." Carter shrugged. "I figured it was my only chance to finally find the real murderer and clear myself."

"The police could have handled the investigation," Kim said softly.

Carter slanted her a wary look. "Like they investigated the murder they hung me for?" he said sarcastically. "Forgive me, Kim, but I don't have any faith in cops. Not after they railroaded me into a life sentence."

"What about the guard?" Brandon asked. "Did you shoot him?"

"No," Carter said. "I tried to stop Morris from killing him." Carter made a disgusted sound in his throat.

Brandon cleared his throat. "Hopefully the guard will regain consciousness and verify your story."

Doubt filled Carter's eyes. "Maybe, but I can't wait on that. I have to find out who killed that private investigator. When he came to see me, I gave him a photo of the woman I was with the night of the murder five years ago. He was trying to track her down."

Kim cleared her throat. "You think your case was the reason he was killed?"

Carter nodded.

Brandon shifted on the balls of his feet. "Listen, Carter, just lie low until we find Lucy, then I'll help you track down this woman."

"I can't wait," Carter said. "If the police find me, I'll go back and rot in jail." A sardonic smile curved his mouth, a remnant of the old devilish Carter. "That is, if they don't kill me first."

Kim reached out and stroked Carter's arm. "Please, turn yourself in, Carter. We'll hire another investigator."

"It's too late for that," Carter said. "I have to find this woman and clear myself."

Brandon and Kim exchanged worried looks. "But it's dangerous," Kim said.

Carter chuckled bitterly. "So is prison. This is my last chance and I'm taking it." Carter pivoted to leave, but Brandon caught him.

"Wait, man. What can I do to help?"

Carter stared at him, the memories of the two of them tussling and fighting and defending each other as kids flashing in Brandon's head. The fact that Carter didn't trust him spoke volumes for their relationship, but somehow the atrocities of their childhood still connected them.

"You can't," Carter said matter-of-factly. "You have to take care of Kim and find your daughter. They need you, Brandon."

Brandon's chest heaved with a sudden ache for Carter and all he'd lost. "At least let me give you some money to help you while you're hiding out."

Carter's expression flattened. "I don't want your charity."

Brandon frowned. "It's not charity. It's one cowboy lending a hand to another."

"The cowboy code," Carter muttered.

Brandon nodded.

"All right," Carter said. "But somehow I'll pay you back."

Brandon shrugged. "When you get your own spread built up, you can send me some steaks."

Kim pressed a hand to Carter's cheek. "Please be careful, Carter. Lucy needs her uncle Carter."

A sea of sadness seemed to wash over Carter; then he pulled Kim into a hug. "You find her while I clear up this mess, then I'll be there to watch her back growing up just like I did yours."

Kim nodded, and Brandon saw tears in her eyes as she pulled away.

Once the four of them, he, Johnny, Carter and Kim, had banded together in friendship and love, all underdogs struggling against the odds.

They would do the same to find his daughter.

KIM WATCHED CARTER drive away in one of Brandon's old pickup trucks with a sick knot in her stomach. Carter hadn't abducted Lucy.

So who had? And where was she?

"Do you think it was wise to give him your truck?" Kim asked. "If the police discover you helped him, they could arrest you for aiding and abetting an escaped felon."

"I couldn't *not* help him," Brandon said. "He's been through hell. And how can I blame him for wanting to clear his name?"

Kim wanted to argue that he should trust the system, but Carter was right. It had failed him miserably just as everyone in his life had.

Even she and Johnny and Brandon had doubted him at a time when he'd needed them most.

"I'm going to call Johnny and fill him in about Carter," Brandon said. "And I'll let the sheriff know that Carter didn't kidnap Lucy."

While he stepped into his office to make the call, she flipped on the TV. Instantly her nerves spiked as the story about Carter and the other escaped prisoners aired.

Then the news replayed her interview.

Images of Lucy rose in her mind, and she rushed outside to the porch, then slumped into the porch swing and looked across the ranch.

"Where are you, baby?" she whispered.

The next few hours dragged by, each second a reminder that Lucy might be in danger. That she could be anywhere in the States. And Texas bordered Mexico... If the kidnapper had crossed the border, they might never find Lucy.

Brandon busied himself on the phone with his accountant again, liquidating more funds, reviewing employee files for possible enemies. Then he and Kim met with the employees and Brandon offered a reward for information.

Suddenly everyone was a suspect. Kim racked her brain for past acquaintances, maintenance workers and vendors she'd met on the Bucking Bronc when they'd worked on the rodeo, for anyone who had seemed unusually interested in her daughter. Every twig that cracked, every rustle of the leaves, every car engine that sounded in the distance made her jump.

She and Brandon decided to ride the ranch once more and look for any clues they might have missed. As they passed the pond, she remembered the picnic she and Brandon and Lucy had shared, the joy on Lucy's face when Brandon had waded in the edge of the water with her. The wildflowers she'd picked and tucked in Lucy's ponytail.

Hours later, she felt drained and exhausted as they returned to the stable and brushed down the horses.

Brandon had been deadly quiet as well.

Finally she finished grooming the palomino and gave him some fresh water and food, then stepped outside the barn and walked back to the porch. Brandon followed close behind. Her legs felt leaden as she climbed the stairs and sank back into the swing.

Brandon moved toward her and started to speak, but her cell phone jangled, and they both froze.

Her hand shook as she stabbed the connect button. "Hello."

"Listen carefully," a computerized voice said. "I have your daughter."

Chapter Eleven

Brandon's stomach churned at the stricken look on Kim's face. He leaned in close to hear the caller.

"Where is she?" Kim cried. "Let me speak to her."

"Just shut up and listen. I want a million dollars. And if you call the police, I will kill your daughter."

Kim crumpled against him, her face ashen, and he jerked the phone from her. "You want money, you son of a bitch? Then let me speak to Lucy."

"I'll call back with details—"

"You're not getting a dime until we have proof that Lucy is alive," Brandon snapped. "Put her on the phone or I'm hanging up."

"Brandon," Kim shrieked. "No…"

Brandon held his ground. "I said let me speak to her."

A heartbeat of silence followed, and Brandon feared the caller was going to hang up. Then a rattling sound followed, and a low mumble from somewhere in the distance.

"Please." Kim squeezed her hands over Brandon's, hugging the phone between them. "We'll pay you the money. I just want to know my little girl is safe."

Another tense moment, then Lucy's voice echoed

back, tiny and frightened. "Mommy, I w-wants to c-come home."

"Oh, baby…" Kim closed her eyes, heaving with relief as tears spilled over. "I love you. Are you okay?"

Brandon's heart pounded like a stallion racing down the track. "Lucy, it's Daddy. Did he hurt you?"

"I'm okay, Daddy. But I don't wike him. He's a meanie."

A big gulp followed, Lucy swallowing back a sob. The sound wrenched Brandon's heart like nothing ever had.

"Listen, sweetie," Brandon said between clenched teeth. "Just do what he says and Mommy and I will have you back at the ranch soon." He clenched and un-clenched his fists. "Spots misses you and so do we."

Lucy's muffled cry followed; then the caller must have grabbed the phone back, because the computer-ized voice returned.

"You have until sundown to get the money. I'll call back with details on where to make the drop."

"Sundown?" Brandon's pulse clamored as he checked the time. Another minute or two and the police might be able to trace the call. "That's only a few hours away."

"And a million is nothing compared to what you have," the voice said. "Get it or lose your precious Lucy."

Brandon clenched his jaw to keep from cursing. Then the phone clicked into silence, and he slammed his fist on the porch rail and let the ugly words spew. Dammit.

He punched the sheriff's number and asked if they got the trace.

"No, it wasn't long enough," Sheriff McRae said. "Do you have any idea who he is?"

"Not a damn clue," Brandon said.

"Did he say where he wants you to bring the money?"

"No," Brandon said. "Just that he'll call back."

"Let me know when he does and we'll arrange for an officer to make the drop."

Brandon thanked him then hung up and turned to Kim. She looked pale and shaken.

"Did they trace it?" Kim asked.

He shook his head. "He didn't stay on the line long enough."

Kim sagged with disappointment.

Brandon pulled her to him and enveloped her in a hug. "When I find this bastard, I'm going to kill him."

"Not if I see him first," Kim said, anger mingling with the fear nearly choking her. "Anyone who would frighten a child like this doesn't deserve to live."

Brandon stroked her back, rocking her in his arms. "No, he needs to suffer."

"A million dollars." Kim sighed, sucking back more tears. "Do you have that much cash available?"

"Not yet, but I've been putting it together. I'll call my accountant and tell him I'll be there by noon to pick it up."

Kim squeezed his shoulder. "Thank you, Brandon."

He arched his brows, his voice hard. "You don't have to thank me, Kim. Lucy is my daughter. I'd do anything to protect her."

Regret filled Kim. "I'm sorry. I should have told you about her sooner."

The hurt in his eyes compounded her guilt. "We

both made mistakes, Kim. Right now let's just focus on the ransom."

Brandon's fierce protectiveness and the conviction in his voice gave her strength.

"The sheriff suggested one of his officers make the drop," Brandon said.

"But we can't risk him hurting Lucy."

"You're right," Brandon said. "It's too risky."

"But what if this is a setup?" Kim asked. "What if the kidnapper runs off with the money and Lucy?"

Brandon stared into her eyes. "We can't think like that," he said. "We heard Lucy's voice. She's scared, but she's all right. We *will* get her back."

Kim struggled to hang on to his words, but still a sliver of fear seized her.

He removed his cell phone from the clip on his belt, and she paced to the window and stared out as she waited on him to make the call. Tonight.

Sundown.

She would bring Lucy home.

She had to.

She couldn't survive another day without having her little girl back in her arms.

BRANDON STEPPED OUTSIDE and dragged in fresh air as he addressed his accountant. "How much did you put together?"

"A half million."

Brandon had explained the reason he needed the money but sworn the man to secrecy. "See how fast you can get me another half. Meanwhile, I'll call Johnny."

He hung up, then punched in Johnny's number. "We received a ransom call."

"Did you talk to Lucy? Is she all right?"

"She's scared but alive."

"Thank God." Johnny sighed heavily. "Did you recognize the voice?"

"No, it was altered, computerized."

Johnny cursed. "What else did he say?"

"He's calling back tonight with the details for making the drop. And he wants a million."

"He expects you to put that much together by tonight?"

"Apparently." Brandon clenched his jaw. "I just talked to my accountant and he has a half million ready."

"I'll handle the rest," Johnny offered. "Just let me make a call, and I'll meet you at the BBL this afternoon."

"Thanks, Johnny. I'll pay you back."

"No way," Johnny said. "This is my niece, Brandon. I want her home the same as you and Kim."

Brandon forgot his anger with Johnny over keeping Lucy from him. He had to. At the moment nothing mattered except his daughter. "I'll see you in a couple of hours." Brandon hung up and went to tell Kim that he was leaving.

He found her on the porch swing hugging Lucy's lamb to her.

"I'm going into San Antonio to pick up the cash," Brandon said. "Johnny's meeting me at the BBL with the other half."

Kim stood. "I'm going with you."

Brandon brushed her elbow with his hand. "Kim, maybe you should stay here and rest."

"I can't rest," Kim said. "I want to be with you."

Brandon hesitated. He wished she wanted to be with him. But he understood her comment came from fear.

She'd been attacked twice. What if the kidnapper was working with a partner and waiting to find Kim alone and vulnerable?

That thought gave him pause and made him rethink the kidnapping. Carter obviously hadn't abducted Lucy. And if someone wanted Lucy for the ransom, why had he or she tried to run the two of them off the road?

He had to look at the situation differently. Figure out who wanted to hurt him.

Kim looked pale as they headed to his SUV, and she remained silent during the drive. She waited in the reception area while he stepped inside his accountant's office to retrieve the bag of cash. They still had an hour to go before meeting Johnny.

Knowing Kim hadn't eaten anything since the day before, he stopped at a barbecue restaurant and led her inside to a table.

"I'm not hungry," Kim said. She'd slipped into a quiet numbness that worried him more than her crying had. Because he shared her fears.

God knows, he'd read enough horror stories in the news about child kidnapping rings and children being sold into foreign countries to not imagine the worst. Texas was too close to the Mexican border for comfort....

"Kim, you look pale and I know you haven't slept much." He waved to the waitress to bring over menus. "If we're going to make it through this and be there for Lucy, we have to eat."

Kim's flat gaze met his. "I just want her back, Brandon."

He felt her pain as if it were his own. "I know. So do I."

He reached across the table and cradled her hand in

his, and for a moment they simply clung to each other, a mother and father both terrified and aching for their missing daughter.

But the waitress intruded with water for both of them. He ordered iced tea and two barbecue plates and they fell into a strained silence. When the food arrived, Kim picked at the sandwich, but she managed to eat the cup of Brunswick stew. He wasn't hungry either, but he wolfed his down anyway just to replenish his energy. He hadn't slept either, and the fear and adrenaline rush that had come with the call was waning as doubts set in.

His mind kept ticking off questions about who wanted to hurt him. He had bought out several small ranchers when he'd been expanding his spread, but most of them had been in financial straits and had welcomed his offer. Marty had balked at the idea of the divorce at first, but between the divorce settlement and her family wealth, she certainly wouldn't need ransom money. Besides, he'd heard she'd been sleeping with some bigwig lawyer already. Photographs of the two of them had been plastered all over the papers. Rumors hinted that an engagement was imminent.

The waitress appeared again, a pencil jammed in her bird's-nest hair. "You want anything else, sugar? We have hot apple pie and a blackberry cobbler to die for."

"No, thanks. Do you want dessert, Kim?"

"No, let's just go."

He paid the check; then they both visited the rest-room before driving to the BBL. When they arrived, Brandon parked in front of Kim's cabin to wait on Johnny. He looked out at the teens Brody had brought in to train as junior counselors and saw himself at that age. Kim had come here to help these boys, another thing they had in common. He wanted to bring her back with Lucy.

Kim checked her watch a half dozen times. "He said he'd call at sundown."

Brandon took her hand. Her skin felt icy, her fingers limp. "Hang in there, Kim. We overcame a lot of obstacles growing up. We'll get through this now."

Kim looked up at him with such big, sad, frightened eyes that he pulled her against him and wrapped his arms around her.

He had let her down once before.

He would never let her down again.

KIM TRIED TO CLING to optimism, but every hour that ticked by, she grew more agitated. She had come to the BBL to start a new life for her and her daughter. She had loved ranch life so much growing up that she'd wanted Lucy to grow up on a ranch, as well.

She'd thought helping the boys would be worthy.

And serve as a good example for Lucy.

Now Lucy was gone....

By the time Johnny arrived, she had chewed off three nails and had a splitting headache.

Johnny took one look at her, handed his duffel bag to Brandon, and hauled her in his arms. "It's going to be okay, Kim. Brandon and I will get Lucy back."

She wanted to trust and believe him. But as much as Brandon meant what he'd said, he might not be able to keep his promise to save their daughter.

Johnny pulled back and looked at her. "You have faith, sis, okay?"

"I'm trying," she whispered.

"Do you want me to go with you and Brandon?"

A protective gleam flashed in Brandon's eyes.

"No," Kim said, "we'll let you know when he calls again."

Johnny released her; then she and Brandon climbed into the car and headed back toward the Woodstock Wagoneer. They passed a group of boys working some cutting horses and Kim thought about Lucy's excitement over Spots. Her head pulsed with a throbbing intensity that made her nauseated, so she closed her eyes.

Images of the past four years rolled through her head. Lucy learning to crawl. Lucy eating her first birthday cupcake, smearing chocolate ice cream in her red hair. Lucy's first Easter egg hunt when she'd had no clue that she was supposed to hunt the eggs. She'd run past them, focused on a wildflower in the yard.

Lucy's sweet voice saying Mama for the first time.

Lucy finally meeting her daddy.

By the time they arrived at Brandon's ranch, the sun had slid downward in the sky, streaking the horizon in a rainbow of oranges, reds and yellows. It was a beautiful sunset, but Kim couldn't feel any joy because she had no idea where Lucy was or what was happening to her. Was she locked in a dark closet somewhere? Had the kidnapper tied her up?

Was he giving her food and water?

Brandon parked in front of the house and cut the engine, then sat and looked out at the ranch for a moment, his jaw set firmly as they watched the sun fade below the tops of the trees.

Sundown.

She clenched her phone with a white-knuckled grip and stared at it, willing it to ring.

BRANDON SET THE DUFFEL BAGS of money inside the kitchen and tossed his keys on the counter just as Kim's cell phone jangled. Her hand jerked as she connected the call.

"Hello."

"Do you have the money?" The computerized voice sounded cold and unfeeling.

"Yes," Kim said between clenched teeth. "Where do we make the exchange?"

"Be quiet and listen carefully." The voice recited the address of a farm. "There's an abandoned storage barn on the east side of the property by the creek. Leave the money in the barn, then drive away. Once I have the cash, I'll call you and tell you where to pick up your little girl."

"No!" Kim cried. "Give her to me when I hand over the money."

"You want her back alive, then do as I say." A brief pause. "And you'd better come alone. No cops. No cowboy heroes. If I suspect someone followed you, you'll never see your precious Lucy again."

Chapter Twelve

Kim's pulse thumped wildly as she disconnected the call and turned to Brandon. She had to leave. She wasn't exactly sure how to find this place and she didn't want to get lost.

"Where are your keys, Brandon?"

Brandon covered her hand with his. "I'll drive, Kim."

"No." She jerked away and snatched the keys. "He said to come alone or he'd hurt Lucy."

Brandon trapped both of her arms this time, stopping her before she could reach for the money. "Kim, there's no way in hell you're meeting this bastard by yourself."

Panic stabbed at Kim. "Do you want to get our daughter killed?"

His eyes narrowed to menacing slits. "You know I don't. I love Lucy, Kim. But you said earlier that the kidnapper might be setting a trap. What if he's luring you there to kill you?"

Kim trembled with anger and fear. "That's a chance I have to take. He asked for money, and I'm delivering it. I'll call you when I have Lucy."

"No." Brandon's harsh tone made Kim draw back.

"The maniac who took Lucy has tried to kill you twice. I swore to you and to Johnny that I'd protect you and Lucy, and I will."

"You can protect Lucy, but you don't owe me anything," Kim shot back. "You gave up that right when you married Marty."

Remorse flickered in his eyes, but he didn't waver. "Maybe so. But we have a daughter together and you're stuck with me. I don't want her to grow up without a mother like I did."

Guilt clawed at her. Brandon had had a terrible childhood. His father had beat him to a pulp while his mother had drank herself to death. Then his father had set the house on fire one night when he'd been doped up on pills and passed out with a cigarette in his mouth. Brandon had rescued his sister but hadn't been able to save his old man. Then he'd assumed responsibility for Joanie.

She released a labored breath. "Brandon, I appreciate your concern, but we can't risk Lucy's life. If the kidnapper sees you and hurts her, I'll never forgive myself." *Or you.*

"He won't see me," Brandon said. "I promise. I'll hide in the back. But I will be there in case he ambushes you."

Kim hesitated. She would feel safer with Brandon backing her up.

He strode to the desk in the corner of the kitchen, unlocked it, then removed a pistol and tucked it into the back of his jeans. Her pulse quickened as he shoved extra ammunition in his pocket, then picked up the bag of cash.

"Okay, now we're ready."

Kim inhaled a deep breath. Then he handed her the

keys and they walked outside to his SUV. Brandon stowed the cash in the backseat, then crawled on the floor and covered himself with a blanket.

Kim plugged the address into the GPS, then switched on the engine and shifted into gear. Anxiety knotted her shoulders, but hope and adrenaline pulsed through her.

She was on her way to bring her daughter home.

And nothing was going to stop her.

BRANDON HAD A BAD PREMONITION as Kim drove toward the drop site.

Something about that address sounded familiar, too, as if he might have been there before. The SUV hit a bump in the road, and he gritted his teeth. He removed his cell phone and tried to google the address, but his battery was low and all he got was static.

Dammit. Why did the address seem familiar?

Had he looked at the land to invest in at some point?

No…he didn't think so. It was north of San Antonio and miles from his ranch, so he would have had no use for it.

Then again, there might be no rhyme or reason for the address other than the fact that it was probably deserted and no cops would be snooping around.

The SUV ate up the miles, the tension in the car palpable. Every breath that Kim took seemed to rattle in the awkward silence.

More questions pounded through his head. The kidnapper had instructed her to leave the money, then he would call with instructions.

But Brandon could not let him leave. If he did, they might never see Lucy again.

Sweat beaded on his skin and trickled down the back

of his shirt. The air in the SUV felt hot and clammy, tires churning over gravel and rock as Kim veered off the main highway.

"Keep alert," Brandon said. "Do you see any cars or a house?"

"No," Kim said in a strained voice. "It looks like this place might have been a working ranch at one time, but it's run-down now."

"How about any barns or other outbuildings?"

"Not yet." Kim sighed. "We're on a long winding drive. It's cloudy and so dark I can barely see."

"Let me know if you spot anything suspicious," Brandon said.

"You think someone is watching us?" Kim asked.

"I don't know. It's possible, especially if the kidnapper has a partner."

"Oh, God…" Kim whispered. "I'll be so glad when this is over."

So would he. He just prayed it ended the way they wanted, with Lucy riding home with them safe and sound. When they had her back, he'd move heaven and hell to track down the person responsible for terrorizing them and make him pay.

The lowlife would be begging for Brandon to call the sheriff rather than face the punishment he would dole out.

Kim swung the SUV to the right and shifted gears, and he held on as the vehicle bounced over several rough patches.

"There's an old barn up ahead," she said, slowing.

"Look around, Kim. Do you see any other buildings? A car in a wooded area? Lights?"

Time ticked by excruciatingly slowly as he waited on her response. Finally she released a pent-up breath. "I don't see anything. It's dark and deserted. Weeds have overtaken the barn and are half covering the door."

"Drive around the outside and look for someone hiding around back?"

"Okay." He gripped the bottom of the seat as she swerved, bouncing again over the weed-infested path. Suddenly she screeched to a halt.

Brandon tensed. "What's wrong?"

"The grass is knee-high," Kim said, sounding weary. "And it looks snake-infested."

"Then drive back around front. I don't want you to get out here."

The SUV jolted him as she backed up and spun the vehicle around. "Brandon, there's an old farmhouse on the hill above the barn. It looks deserted, but he could be holding Lucy there."

Brandon itched to sit up and search the area himself. He hated to think of Kim climbing out in an overgrown snake bed with a dangerous kidnapper watching. Maybe even waiting to attack her.

"I'm going to put the money in the barn like he instructed," Kim said in a shaky voice.

"Wait," Brandon said. "Unlock the glove compartment and take my other pistol."

"Brandon—"

"You need protection, Kim. And if you see or hear anything, shoot."

Kim's nervous breath echoed through the car. "I will."

"Reach under the seat and grab a flashlight, too," Brandon whispered.

He heard her shifting as she felt for one, then saw a light flicker on. Then the sound of the car door lock clicking made him catch his breath, and he held it while Kim climbed out.

He closed his eyes and prayed again as she shut the door and left him inside. Dammit, he felt helpless and more terrified than he'd ever felt in his life.

KIM'S HANDS SHOOK as she clutched the duffel bag of money and plowed her way toward the barn. She was grateful she'd worn boots because the weed-infested brush was knee-high and obliterated the trail that had once led to the drive. Wind whistled through the trees, shaking and rattling them, the smell of damp moss and rotting wood swirling around her.

The kidnapper couldn't have Lucy here. Could he?

What if he had left her inside that snake hole?

Her heart beat so loudly that she heard the blood roaring in her ears. "Lucy?" She picked her way over loose rocks and dirt clumps, shining the flashlight to guide her way.

Grass and weeds clawed at her jeans, and she stumbled over a rock, nearly slipping into some scrub brush. But she caught herself and pushed aside a patch of weeds in front of the barn door, then pulled hard to open the door.

Rotting wood splintered in her hands and the bottom of the door dug into the dirt, but she managed to wedge it open just enough to peer inside.

"Lucy?"

Nothing but the wind whistling again, and in the distance, the wail of a vulture.

She shined the flashlight across the interior of the barn, shivering as she noticed more weeds, broken-down, rusty farm equipment and a pitchfork propped against the wall. A window was broken out near the right side, and leaves and dust swirled inside.

Lucy wasn't inside though, so she dropped the money and turned to head back to the SUV.

Suddenly a shot rang out. Kim darted sideways as the bullet whizzed by her head.

Then another shot pinged off the barn door, and she screamed and ducked down into the trees, searching blindly for the shooter. Inside, she heard something moving.

Then running.

Someone had been hiding inside that barn.

And now he was escaping with the money....

BRANDON'S PULSE JUMPED at the sound of the gunshots ringing out. He grabbed his gun and swung open the car door, searching for Kim. Dear God, had the shooter killed her?

The air felt thick and muggy; the night was dark and cloudy. He scanned the weeds surrounding the barn and thought he saw movement. Then another shot blasted from the right, and he spotted a figure in the woods.

He fired back, ducking low as he ran for the barn. "Kim?"

"By the door," she whispered.

He released another shot to ward off the shooter. "Are you hit?" he shouted.

"No, but he's escaping with the money."

"I'll go after him." Brandon pushed to his feet, still ducking low as he ran toward the woods. But the sound of a motor rent the air, and he looked up and saw a motorbike zipping through the woods. He ran faster, desperately trying to get a look at the driver, then realized he couldn't catch him or her on foot and his SUV wouldn't make it through the woods.

Dammit.

A ray of moonlight shimmered off the trees where the bike headed, and he cursed again. There were two people on the bike.

They had been working together. One had snuck into the barn to retrieve the money while the other fired at Kim.

Had they intended to scare her, or had they been trying to kill her?

Heart pounding, he fired a round toward the shooter, but he was too far away to hit him. His boots crushed dry brush as he hurried to Kim, but by the time he reached her, she was running toward him.

He pointed to the woods. "The kidnapper escaped on a motorcycle."

Kim clutched his arm. "Could you see who it was? Did he have Lucy with him?"

"No, they were too far away," Brandon said. "And there were two people, but they were both adults."

Kim sagged against him. "So where's Lucy?"

He had no idea, but terrifying thoughts bombarded him. The property was overgrown, deserted, had been abandoned for months probably, maybe longer. And there were too many places to hide a body....

He could not share those fears with Kim though.

So he scanned the property and noticed the old farmhouse Kim had mentioned. "Let's check out the house. Maybe they left her inside."

A flicker of hope, then terror flickered in Kim's eyes, and he realized he hadn't had to voice his worst fears. Kim was thinking the same thing.

The kidnapper could have killed Lucy and buried

her here or left her in that house and was getting farther and farther away.

They hurried back to the SUV, and this time Brandon drove, speeding up the dusty trail and sending rocks flying behind the wheels. His headlights beamed down on overgrown grass and brush that had choked the life out of the land, his anxiety mounting with each second.

They bounced over a pothole, then screeched to a stop a few feet from the house, the headlights highlighting the chipped, peeling paint and rotting wood. Kim reached for the door handle and he covered her hand. "Let me go first. Stay behind me and keep alert."

Someone could still be inside, waiting to strike. They might be walking into a trap that the kidnapper had set and end up dead.

Then they'd never know what happened to their daughter.

KIM TRIED TO CONTROL her panic by taking deep breaths as she and Brandon wove their way up the dirt path to the front porch of the old farmhouse. The porch was sagging, boards broken and cracked, and one of the posts had splintered. The shutters on the house hung askew, weathered and worn from storms, and mud caked the house.

The thought of her little girl in this creepy place sent a shiver down her spine.

She had seen the terror in Brandon's eyes as well. He was afraid the kidnapper had killed Lucy and left her here for them to find.

Or worse…left her body in the woods.

Shuddering with revulsion at the thought, she silently willed herself to remain positive. The kidnapper had said he'd call with Lucy's location once he picked up the money. She had to believe that would happen.

The door squeaked as Brandon pushed it open, and Kim glanced behind her to make sure the shooter hadn't returned. He could have parked the bike in the woods again and sneaked back to the house.

A musty odor mingled with mildew and something else Kim couldn't define—maybe rancid food or a dead animal—assaulted her as Brandon eased one foot inside the door. The linoleum squeaked beneath his boots, and he shined the flashlight across the room, revealing scarred dingy walls, a broken kitchen table, a counter caked with layers of grime, and then something else that made Kim's pulse race.

Fast-food wrappers.

Someone had been here recently.

Brandon strode over, picked up the bag and sniffed. "Fresh. Burgers and fries."

Kim's heart jumped. "Lucy loves French fries."

Brandon's dark gaze met hers in the weak moonlight pouring through the old house. Somewhere outside a wild animal, maybe a coyote, howled. The wind whistled through the eaves, rattling broken windows and sending a chill through the room.

Brandon clenched the flashlight and gestured toward a door leading to another room. He held the gun in one hand, braced and ready while Kim pushed open the door, her own weapon clenched, ready to fire to protect him.

Darkness bathed the living room, but it was so quiet she heard Brandon's labored breathing. The foul odor grew stronger, and he waved the flashlight across the room, a beam of light illuminating a dead rat in the corner.

She cringed. An orange-and-green flowered sofa sat lopsided with one of its feet missing, and stuffing pouring out where it appeared birds had picked at it.

Then the flashlight zoned in on the floor.

Kim lost her breath as she spotted the dark crimson stain. It was blood. A pool of it.

And right beside it lay a hair ribbon.

The yellow ribbon Lucy had been wearing when she'd been abducted.

Chapter Thirteen

Blood…a lot of it.

Brandon clenched his fist, praying it wasn't Lucy's. It couldn't be. She had to be alive.

Kim's pained gasp jerked his attention to her, and she stooped to touch the ribbon, but he yanked her hand back. "Don't. We'll need forensics to examine it."

But she gathered the hair ribbon in her hand anyway, clinging to it. "This is Lucy's. She was here."

A shaky sigh echoed in the air, and he rubbed Kim's back. "Stay put. I'm going to check the rest of the house."

Kim nodded silently, but her gaze remained rooted to the dark stain on the floor.

"Kim," he said, helping her stand. "Honey, stay alert. They could have set a trap and be coming back." Although he doubted it. He had a feeling the kidnappers were roaring away, celebrating their coup.

His words snapped Kim from her shock. She removed the pistol from the back of her jeans, pressed her back against the wall and faced the doorway as if to watch for trouble. He wielded his gun as he moved through the bottom floor. The two bedrooms were small and practically empty except for a cot in one room with a threadbare blanket and a pillow that smelled like dust and mold. Rat droppings littered the corners and holes in the wooden floor suggested termites had infested the wood.

Anger surged through him. Had the kidnapper brought Lucy here and made her sleep in this filthy room? Had he hurt her? Or worse…

No, he couldn't allow himself to believe that. Surely God wouldn't let him discover he had a daughter and lose her in the same week?

Again, he considered the address. It might offer a lead, so he hurried back to the living room. Kim was still frozen in the corner, her face ashen, her hands trembling as she gripped the gun.

Her cell phone trilled, and she startled, her terrified gaze meeting his.

He hurried toward her, then took her gun as she snagged the phone. He checked the caller ID with her, but it registered unknown.

Maybe this was the kidnapper with directions where they could pick up their daughter. He prayed that was the case. But the computerized voice made his blood turn to ice.

"I warned you to come alone. Now you can forget about ever seeing Lucy."

The phone clicked into silence. Brandon groaned and caught Kim as she broke into a sob and sagged into his arms.

KIM DOUBLED OVER, the pain unbearable. Had the killer punished Lucy to teach her a lesson?

"You shouldn't have come," Kim wailed. "This is my fault, your fault. If he hurt Lucy…"

Brandon closed his arms around her, his big body

offering strength and redemption. But she didn't deserve redemption, not if she had gotten Lucy killed by disobeying the kidnapper's instructions.

"Kim, he's bluffing," Brandon said. "Think about it. How did he know I was there? I didn't show myself until after he opened fire on you."

Kim cried out, beating her fists against him. "Maybe he had someone else watching the ranch or he had cameras." On some level, she realized she sounded irrational, but she couldn't help herself.

Brandon stroked her back, soothing her with whispered words, and she clung to him, afraid she'd collapse if he didn't hold her up.

"Come on, let's get out of here," he murmured. "I have to call Johnny."

"Why?" Kim shuddered against him. "Johnny can't help us now."

"We have to regroup," Brandon said. "Figure out who's behind this."

She pulled back to look up at him although her eyes were so blurred with tears she could barely see his face. "I've been wracking my brain trying to figure that out. Before she was kidnapped, no one knew Lucy was your child but me and Johnny. And I can't think of anyone who'd want to hurt me."

Brandon coaxed her outside to the SUV. The night air shifted around her, steeped with the ugly violence that might have occurred here tonight. She could have sworn she heard her little girl's cries echoing in the whistling wind.

"I'll examine my employee files again," Brandon said. "If it's about my money, maybe I missed something."

Numb, she hunched in the SUV as Brandon drove away from the deserted house.

Brandon punched in Johnny's number as he veered onto the main road. "We made the drop, but someone shot at Kim. I fired back, but the kidnapper escaped." A pause. "Yes, Kim's all right, but the kidnapper called and said... Well, he didn't tell us where Lucy was. He implied we wouldn't see her again."

"God," Johnny muttered.

"And, Johnny, there were two of them working as a team. One shot at Kim while the other retrieved the money."

Kim stared at her phone, willing it to ring again.

But she had angered the kidnapper now, and there was no telling what he might do to her little girl.

"Listen, Johnny, something about this area seemed familiar. I just realized that I looked at it when I was researching land for Brody for the Bucking Bronc Lodge, but decided not to bid on it. The owner was in financial trouble then. I don't know if he sold it or not, but it's worth investigating."

Another hesitation. "We could use a P.I. to run a background check on the owner. When I get home, I'll text you the guy's information."

"All right. I'll call Aiden Hollister."

Brandon's loud sigh punctuated the air. "Maybe this guy was pissed because I didn't bail him out of financial trouble, so he kidnapped Lucy for the money to save himself."

Brandon hung up, then turned to Kim. "It's a long shot, but it might be a lead."

"If that's the case," Kim said, grasping to follow his logic, "why would he attack me at the Bucking Bronc?

It's not like you and I have been together for the past few years. Why not just come after you?"

Brandon shrugged. "He needed leverage. Maybe he followed me to the Bucking Bronc and knew about my investment."

"Still, why attack me? Why not abduct your wife?"

"I don't know. Because we were divorced, I guess." Brandon's fingers tightened around the steering wheel. "Maybe he knew we'd been together in the past? Or hell, maybe somehow he discovered that Lucy was mine. You said only you and Johnny knew. But what about the doctor and hospital staff?" Frustration sharpened his voice. "Did you put my name on Lucy's birth certificate?"

She knotted her hands in her lap. "Yes. I…listed you as the father. I…thought if anything ever happened to me, if there were medical issues, it was important."

"God, Kim, you don't have to make excuses," Brandon said through gritted teeth. "I am her father. I'd be pissed if you hadn't listed me."

Her mind spun with questions. Had someone been looking for a way to blackmail Brandon and seen that birth certificate and decided it was their ticket to his fortune?

TENSION THRUMMED through the SUV as Brandon closed the distance to the ranch. Kim had disappeared into a sullen silence that worried him.

He couldn't help but blame himself and wondered if she was blaming him, too. Not that he regretted accompanying her tonight. If he hadn't, Kim might be dead.

The shooting had been a ploy to distract her while the accomplice confiscated the money. Either that, or someone really wanted her dead.

But who would want to hurt her? She'd insisted she didn't have any enemies. No past boyfriends.

Except for him.

Which meant the kidnapping *had* been intended to hurt him.

"Kim, think back. Was there anyone at the hospital who seemed suspicious?"

"That was over four years ago, Brandon. It was traumatic, but nothing sticks out. Everyone was there to help deliver Lucy." She sighed and ran a hand through her hair. "Besides, if someone wanted to use her to get to you, why wait four years?"

Brandon stewed over that question. "You're right. That doesn't make sense." He veered around a curve and passed a slow trucker. "So, maybe the guy who owned this land got desperate and decided to look into my past and see if there was something he could use to blackmail me. He discovered I was divorced, so wrote off kidnapping Marty. Besides, tackling the Canterberry family would have been daunting and garnered major national publicity." He chewed the inside of his cheek. "So, he does some digging. Finds out you and I had a relationship in the past. Learns you had a baby and never married." His gaze shot to hers, the pieces clicking into place. "He finds a way to sneak a peek at the birth certificate, and hits pay dirt."

Kim nodded, her expression grave. "I suppose that's possible."

The Woodstock Wagoneer came into view, and the ramifications of failing slammed into him. When he'd left earlier, he'd expected to be bringing Lucy home tonight. To cuddle her and tuck her into her own bed.

Kim kept twisting Lucy's hair ribbon around her fingers as he parked and they went inside.

"I'm going to find that ranch owner's name and contact the P.I. to track him down for us," Brandon said as he flipped on the kitchen light. "And I'll let the sheriff know our suspicions."

Kim nibbled on her bottom lip. "But what if it's too late?"

He rubbed her arms. "Don't give up. There's still a chance the kidnapper will call. And if he doesn't…"

"Then what?" Kim cried.

"Then I'll track him down. The Amber alert is out. The story is still airing. We'll call in the feds to escalate the search." He injected determination into his voice. "We will find her, Kim. I won't give up until we do."

She nodded, then turned and climbed the steps to the bedroom. Knowing it was going to be a long night, he made a pot of coffee, then carried a mug to his office and began digging through his files.

When he'd worked with Marty's father, he had also viewed properties for him, including this one, but Marty had been appalled at the conditions and had convinced him not to purchase it. He'd looked at dozens of properties for himself before buying the first three hundred acres of his ranch; then he'd had to wheel and deal and buy out other neighboring ranchers to expand. But that piece hadn't fit his needs then either. There had been no water source and too many problems with the soil.

Then he'd suggested it to Brody for the Bucking Bronc Lodge, but Brody had already found a better property, one more suited to the camps they'd planned and more accessible to town.

He finally located the man's name—Herbert Baxter—then tried the phone number listed on the file, but it had been disconnected. A quick Google search led to nothing.

He phoned Johnny. "The owner of the property was a man named Herbert Baxter. The phone number I have has been disconnected."

"I'll ask Hollister to locate him," Johnny said.

Brandon drummed his fingers on the desk. "Thanks." He hesitated. "I'm worried, Johnny. We found blood at the house. These kidnappers...what if they hurt Lucy? Or worse? What if she's not alive and we never find her? He could have left her out there in the woods..."

"Stop it." Johnny made a low sound in his throat. "We will find her and the party responsible. We won't give up until we do."

Brandon heaved a breath. "I'm going to call the sheriff and fill him in. I want the police to analyze that blood and look for other forensics. If the blood belongs to the kidnapper, maybe we can use it to identify him."

"Good thinking," Johnny said. "When we track down the kidnappers, we want to make sure they rot in jail."

Brandon gritted his teeth. They wouldn't make it to jail. He'd kill the lowlifes first.

Johnny hung up, and Brandon punched the sheriff's number. Just as he expected, the sheriff reamed him out for not informing them about the kidnapper's follow-up call.

"How the hell are we supposed to help if you don't keep us informed?" Sheriff McRae bellowed.

"Listen, Sheriff, we couldn't risk Lucy's life," Brandon said, although he wondered if they'd made a mistake by not calling the police. "The kidnapper was angry enough that I accompanied Kim. If he'd seen you, he would have killed her for sure."

The sheriff's labored sigh followed. "You may have to face the fact that he never intended to give Lucy back. That he planned to kill Kim, leave with the money and never contact you again."

"I realize that's a possibility," Brandon said. "But I pray you're wrong." Perspiration beaded on his forehead. "But that's one reason I called. I thought you might check the house and barn for evidence." *And look for a body...*

He couldn't say the words, but the sheriff's grunt indicated he understood.

"I'll send a crime unit out there now," the sheriff said. "You said the shooter fired at Kim by the barn?"

"Yeah. I returned fire, but don't think I hit him."

"Still, we'll look for bullet casings," Sheriff McRae said. "If the guy's weapon is in the system for a prior, we might be able to track him down that way. If not, we can use it later to make an ID and prosecute him when we make an arrest."

"Thanks," Brandon said. Although this SOB might not make it to jail.

"Listen, Woodstock, I'm warning you though. Don't take the law into your own hands. The last thing your little girl will want is to visit you in jail when she gets home."

Brandon clenched his jaw. The sheriff was right. But Kim's cries and Lucy's terrified voice echoed in his head, and he didn't know if he could control his rage if he found the bastard.

He ended the call, then headed up the stairs to check on Kim.

Kim stood at the window of her room looking out, the moonlight a soft halo around her.

He couldn't stand to see her suffer. Moving on adrenaline and too many pent-up emotions, he crossed the room and wrapped his arms around her. She leaned into him, her body shuddering with silent sobs.

He soothed her with whispered nothings and stroked her back, pressing her against him, and she clung to him as if she needed him as much as he needed her.

He had only meant to comfort her, but when she looked up in his eyes, tears glistening on her lashes and hunger flaring, raw and hot in her gaze, he lowered his head and claimed her mouth with his.

KIM ACHED FROM THE INSIDE OUT. She was terrified she would never see Lucy again. It was selfish for her to accept comfort from Brandon, but he was Lucy's father, and they had made Lucy together.

And he was hurting, too. She could see it in his dark sexy eyes, and feel it in the way his big body shook.

They were Lucy's parents and they had to cling to each other or they wouldn't survive.

His tongue probed her lips apart, and she succumbed to the need to taste him and pulled him closer, savoring the hungry sound he made in his throat as he deepened the kiss. Their tongues mated and danced together as he threaded his fingers in her hair and angled her head to explore her more deeply.

She ran her hands over the hard planes of his back, propelled by the need to wrap herself in his masculine strength.

Brandon had always been strong, protective, a tough guy who took care of others, and she needed him now.

He needed her, too. She felt it in the intensity of his

kiss, in the raw hunger emanating from his hands as he traced one down her back, over the column of her spine, to her hips where he pulled her against his hard length. His heated kiss aroused long-dormant sensations to burst within her, and she whispered his name, a plea for more.

He tore his mouth from hers and nibbled at the sensitive shell of her earlobe, then trailed kisses down her neck and throat. She leaned her head back in wild abandon, wanting more, and tore at the buttons on his shirt.

Comfort quickly turned to lust and hunger as they stripped, tossing clothes to the floor in their haste to be closer together. To feel skin against skin, heat against heat, hearts and bodies becoming one.

Brandon made a guttural sound in his throat and backed her toward the bed, then gently eased her onto the mattress. Kim gripped his face between her hands, savoring the desire flickering in his eyes and remembering the first time they'd made love. She'd been young and naive and inexperienced, but he'd been tender and loving.

She didn't want tender now. She wanted his hands and mouth on her, wanted him pumping inside her, wanted him to drive the fear and sadness from her body and make her forget that just for a moment, they were in the midst of a living nightmare.

Brandon brushed his palm against her stomach, and their eyes locked. For a moment, she felt as if they'd slipped back in time and that he could read her mind. That he saw into her soul and knew that she'd never stopped loving him.

That he was the only man she ever would or could love.

Feeling raw and exposed, she lifted one hand and

traced a finger down his chest, over his belly, then south to the throbbing heat pressed against her stomach. Her fingers closed over his thick length, and he growled low and deep, then dipped his head and kissed her again.

Their kisses became frantic, desperate, so passionate that Kim felt her orgasm building, her body begging for sweet release.

Brandon didn't disappoint. He kissed her breasts, tugged one nipple into his mouth and sucked so hard that she nearly came off the bed with a moan. He stroked her other nipple to a turgid peak, then laved it and suckled her, using his free hand to find her heat and slip two fingers inside.

She was wet and aching, and parted her legs in invitation. Brandon stroked her until she was nearly mindless; then he dipped his tongue to the heart of her. She moaned and arched into him, letting him love her as she dug her fingers into his shoulders.

Sensations charged through her body in a quivering rush. Kim cried out his name, and was rewarded when he rose above her and slid his thick length inside her. She gripped his shoulders, losing herself in the energy of their bodies slapping and moving together in a frenetic rhythm.

He lifted her hips, angling her so he could plunge deeper, then filled her so completely that she fell over the edge and her body shook with pleasure as another orgasm ripped through her.

She closed her eyes, battling tears and the words of love that threatened to spill over. She had known making love with Brandon again would mean losing her heart to him.

Then again, she had lost it years ago, and had never reclaimed it.

Chapter Fourteen

Brandon collapsed against Kim, his body sated, his heart aching. How had he ever broken it off with Kim years ago?

Why had he been such a fool?

She snuggled against his chest, and he wrapped his arms around her tighter. He had her back now, and he would never let her go again.

Somehow he'd save their daughter and spend the rest of his life making up to Kim for the pain he'd caused her. He'd love and protect her and Lucy every damn moment of every damn day.

Kim grew still, and he realized she must have fallen asleep. He closed his eyes, and found himself dozing off as well, but an hour later, he jerked awake, his heart racing with worry.

Knowing he wouldn't sleep again, he climbed from bed, grabbed his clothes and went downstairs. He made a pot of coffee, then pored through employee files and past business deals, searching for anyone else he thought might have a grudge against him in case Baxter's property turned out to be a dead end.

Another possibility occurred to him. Maybe the kidnapper wasn't holding a grudge. Maybe he just desperately needed money.

He studied the files again, searching for financial inconsistencies, but personal backgrounds and family information were minimal. His phone buzzed at about 5:30 a.m. and he answered quickly.

"Brandon Woodstock."

"This is Aiden Hollister. I have an address on Baxter."

"Thanks." Brandon scribbled it down. "Listen, if I send over a list of my employees, can you find out if any of them are financially strapped? I'm looking for motive."

"Sure, just email me the list and I'll get on it."

Brandon thanked him, then attached the file and emailed it to Hollister.

Anxious to talk to Baxter, he rushed to his bedroom and showered, then dressed. He peeked in on Kim, but she was resting and he hated to disturb her. So he jotted a note explaining where he was going and asking her to call him immediately if she heard from the kidnapper, then propped it in front of the coffeepot.

Then he retrieved his gun, snatched his keys and headed out to his SUV. The sun was just climbing over the tops of the junipers and oaks as he left the ranch, the temperature heating up to the eighties. It would be a long hot Texas day, and unbearable if they didn't hear about Lucy.

The cattle grazing in the pasture seemed oblivious to his turmoil though, as did the horses galloping freely across the land. The irony struck him. He had a fortune invested in his prized ranch, but nothing meant anything to him now unless he brought his daughter back alive.

The fact that the sheriff hadn't called saying they

had found Lucy on that deserted ranch was a good sign. It had to be.

Stomach knotting at the thought of the blood on the floor though, he punched the gas pedal, the SUV eating the miles between him and Baxter's place in San Antonio.

The city was just coming alive with commuters, buses, tourists and families strolling the sidewalks and pouring into coffee shops and diners as he cut through the downtown streets and found his way to the retirement community called Southwind for Seniors on the northeast part of town.

The community was set on fifty acres with a central inn that offered apartments as well as individual cabins boasting a rustic feel. Natural wooded areas, greenery, lawns and blooming plants made it feel more like a vacation spot than a home for seniors. A pool and recreation area, tennis courts and clubhouse occupied one corner built strategically around man-made waterways. A large pond provided recreation for canoe rides, and picnic tables were scattered along the bank for gatherings.

Nursing facilities and a medical complex also were integral to the community.

It couldn't be cheap to live here. Had Baxter needed money for health care?

He made his way through security, then parked in front of a row of log cabins. Budding flowers and live oaks flanked the rustic front, a sharp contrast to the deserted overgrown property Baxter had left behind.

Brandon tucked his gun beneath his jacket, hoping he wouldn't need to use it, but also hoping this man had answers.

If he didn't, Brandon had no idea where to turn next.

Kɪᴍ ᴡᴏᴋᴇ ᴡɪᴛʜ ᴀ sᴛᴀʀᴛ. She could have sworn she had heard her little girl crying, that she was just across the hall. But reality hit her with the force of a physical blow.

Perspiration beaded on her forehead as she shoved at the comforter and rolled over, searching for Brandon.

He was gone.

Memories of the night before crashed back. The old deserted farmhouse. The blood. The call. Not finding Lucy.

Making love with Brandon.

She'd been starved for comfort, and Brandon had held her in his arms. Her dreams of being with him had suddenly seemed real. Possible.

So why had he left her alone in bed?

Had he heard something about their daughter?

Her pulse raced, and she grabbed her robe and raced down the stairs calling Brandon's name. A quick glance in the kitchen indicated it was empty, so she checked his study. Papers littered his desk, and his computer was on. She glanced at the screen and saw he'd been researching employee files.

A message light revealed he had two new emails. Had he found something? Could the kidnapper have sent a message?

Her hand trembled as she clicked the icon to bring up his mail. The first was a bid on some cattle. The second one was from Marty, Brandon's ex-wife.

Her chest clenched as she read the message.

Dear Brandon,
Please call me, sweetheart. I heard about your daughter being kidnapped and I will do anything I can to help you. I still love you and I know you

love me, too. I can't wait to hold you in my arms again.
Love, your wife forever,
Marty

Jealousy seized Kim, along with sudden fear. Brandon hadn't seen these emails, but he could have been talking to her all along. Had he left her bed to talk to Marty? Was he planning a reconciliation?

Had he slept with Kim out of pity?

And what about Lucy?

How had Marty found out she was Brandon's? Had he called and told her?

Suddenly furious at the thought of him deserting her and her daughter, and at herself for falling into his arms and bed again, she headed toward his bedroom.

"Brandon!"

The door stood ajar so she knocked loudly, then pushed open the door. "Brandon, are you in here?"

She scanned the room, once again surprised that the furnishings were more masculine and that she didn't see touches of Marty in this room.

But Brandon wasn't inside.

A wet towel was draped over the towel bar in the adjoining bathroom, and she realized he had showered.

She rushed to check for his SUV, but it was gone. How could Brandon have left without telling her? What if the kidnapper called?

She would have no way to go meet him.

Unless he had called and Brandon had answered and gone without her....

Her heart stuttered as she rushed to check her phone, but there had been no incoming calls.

She wanted to scream with frustration. Where was he?

Shaking with worry, she stormed back to the kitchen to make a pot of coffee, punching in his number as she grabbed a mug. The call rolled to voice mail, and she slammed her hand on the counter in anger.

Then she spotted the note propped in front of the coffeemaker. Hoping it was good news, she flipped it open.

Kim,
The P.I. called with an address for the owner of that deserted property where we made the drop. Maybe this is the lead we need. Call me if you hear anything.
Brandon

Please let it be a lead.

Relieved to know he was working on finding Lucy instead of with Marty, she poured a cup of coffee. Although disappointment plucked at her as she reread the note. Brandon hadn't said he loved her or even signed *Love, Brandon.* The note had been short and to the point.

Did he regret making love to her? Or had last night just been a night of sex to tide him over until he and his wife solved their differences?

Renewed anger tightened every muscle in her body. How could she have been such a fool to have fallen in love with him again? He'd only been divorced a few months. Did he regret it?

Furious at herself, she carried her coffee to the porch and looked out across the ranch.

When they brought Lucy home safe and sound and the kidnapper was in jail, she and Lucy would move back to the Bucking Bronc Lodge.

She would walk away from Brandon this time with her dignity still intact.

And he would never know that he'd crushed her heart again.

BRANDON STUDIED the wiry-haired older man in the doorway, scrutinizing him for signs he was a vicious kidnapper. But the frail man with his nearly bald head, crooked wire-rimmed glasses and age spots dotting his gnarled hands didn't fit the profile of a criminal.

"Mr. Baxter, I need to talk to you."

A little boy about ten ran up and tugged at the old man's leg. "Grandpa, can we finish the game?"

"In a minute." Mr. Baxter patted the boy's shoulder affectionately. "Why don't you pop some popcorn in the microwave while I find out what this man needs."

Brandon gave the kid a quick smile, his gut instincts telling him this trip was a waste. Then again, maybe Baxter had been desperate for some reason....

"What's going on?" Baxter asked.

Brandon cleared his throat. "I don't know if you saw the news about that little girl, Lucy Long, who was kidnapped."

Baxter pulled at his chin. "Yeah, I saw it. But what's that got to do with me?"

"My name is Brandon Woodstock. A while back I looked at a piece of property you owned outside San Antonio."

Baxter quirked a white brow, confused. "Yeah, but I sold that land last year. Got an offer I couldn't refuse."

"Who did you sell it to?"

"Why do you want to know?"

"The little girl who was kidnapped is my daughter,"

Brandon said. "Yesterday, the kidnapper demanded we bring the ransom money to your old ranch."

Baxter coughed into his hand. "Good lord, I had no idea."

"Being you owned that property, I thought that you might know something about the kidnapping."

Baxter wheezed a breath; then his eyes flickered with sudden understanding. "You thought I had something to do with it?"

Brandon jammed his hands in the pockets of his jeans. "That property is the only lead I have."

The man's gaze latched with his. "Listen to me, Mr. Woodstock. I found out I'm dying last year. That's why I sold my place. It was the best thing I ever did because I've reconnected with my children and grandchildren again." He gestured over his shoulder toward the kitchen.

"There's no way I'd jeopardize my family." He moved to shut the door. "Now, I'm sorry about your daughter. I can't imagine what you're going through, but I had nothing to do with it."

Sincerity echoed in Baxter's tone.

Brandon nodded but caught the door. "All right. But just tell me who bought your land."

The man removed his glasses and rubbed at his eyes. "Sure, hang on and let me get the information."

The little boy yelled for his grandfather, and Baxter told him he'd be right there. A minute later, he returned and handed Brandon a piece of paper with a name on it.

Brandon glanced at the name in confusion. A corporation had bought the land. But who owned the corporation? And what would they have wanted with that property?

He turned and jogged back to his car, disappointment ballooning in his chest. He'd have the P.I. check it out.

But he had a bad feeling it was a dead end. A corporation wouldn't be involved in a child kidnapping. More likely, the kidnapper had stumbled on the deserted property and taken advantage of the isolated location as a hiding spot.

He mentally recounted the events of the past few days as he drove back to the ranch. He had to have missed something.

There were two kidnappers, a team. Kim had been attacked before she'd come to his place, then at his ranch. So far, none of his employees had come forward with information, but maybe Hollister would uncover something about one of them that would prove helpful. Still, he wanted to talk to them himself. Study their faces. See if anyone looked nervous.

He accelerated, anxious to get home, then punched in his ranch foreman's number.

"Walt, have all the hands meet me at the dining hall in an hour. I need to talk to them."

After Walt agreed to spread the word, Brandon phoned the P.I. and gave him the name of the corporation that had bought Hollister's land.

Then he hung up and sped toward the ranch. Kim would be awake by now.

Maybe she had heard something.

ANXIETY KNOTTED EVERY MUSCLE in Kim's body. She paced the kitchen, constantly checking the drive and the phone for Brandon or any updates on Lucy.

Why didn't someone answer her pleas on the news? Where was Lucy? Was she hurt? Did she know that her mother and father were going out of their minds looking for her?

The sound of an engine rumbling down the road made her jump, and she rushed outside on the porch and watched as Brandon appeared. He unfolded his big, hard, lean body from the SUV, and she fought to keep from running toward him and begging him not to go back to Marty.

To make a family with her and Lucy.

But she took one look at his chiseled jaw and swallowed the words. The tight line of his frown suggested he didn't have good news.

"You haven't heard anything?" he asked as he trudged up the porch steps.

She shook her head. "No. What happened?"

"I tracked down the man who used to own the property where we dropped the ransom. He's terminally ill and sold it to a corporation then moved into a retirement community." He scrubbed a hand over his chin. "I'm pretty sure he had nothing to do with the kidnapping."

Kim sagged into the porch swing. "What now?"

"I called Johnny's P.I. friend to check out the corporation. Maybe it's a lead."

Kim tried not to fall apart, but she felt herself losing it. "So we're still in the dark. And Lucy is out there...." She glared at Brandon, the fact that he'd chosen Marty over her and he might do so again, and the tension of not knowing if her daughter was alive, eating at her.

"This is our fault," she said, breaking down. "*My* fault. If I'd taken better care of Lucy, watched her more carefully, if you'd been around, she wouldn't be gone."

"Kim," Brandon said, reaching out to console her.

"We will find her. I'm not giving up and neither can you."

"But you heard what he said. I told you to let me go alone," she shouted. "If I had, I'd have my daughter back now."

Brandon's eyes flared with anger. "No, you'd probably be dead. And then Lucy wouldn't have a mother."

Hysteria bubbled in her chest. "No, I'd have her back, but you insisted on coming and now we may never know where she is." Kim stood, the layers of hurt too much to bear. "Besides, what does it matter to you if I'm dead? You didn't want me and Lucy four years ago. You have a wife—"

"Kim, stop it!" Brandon shouted. "We're going to find Lucy. I promise."

A muscle ticked in his jaw, and Kim knew on some level, she was being unfair. But he'd left her in bed alone, and she'd read that email and all she could see her in mind was that blood…Lucy's blood. And the picture of Marty and Brandon on their wedding day…

"I know how well you keep your promises." She whirled around and ran into the house. A second later, the door slammed, and she heard Brandon's footsteps pound inside.

"I'm not giving up," he said in a gruff voice. "I'm going to meet with my employees again. When I get back, we need to talk."

The door banged shut and tears spilled over, running down her cheeks. She knew he was doing everything he could to find Lucy, but what if it wasn't enough?

Her cell phone buzzed, and her heart jumped as she raced to it and snatched it up.

"Hello."

"You have one more chance," the computerized

voice said. "Bring a hundred thousand in small bills to the address you'll receive on your text. And this time come alone, or you'll find your daughter dead."

Chapter Fifteen

Brandon fought hurt over Kim's comments. He'd thought they had bonded again last night. They'd shared comfort and an incredible night of lovemaking that had only confirmed that they should have been together all along.

But Kim blamed him for losing Lucy and not protecting them and for leaving her years ago, and no matter what he did, he'd never earn her trust again.

Defeat weighed heavily on his chest as he strode into the dining hall to meet his employees. The ranch hands consisted of good old boys and young cowboys who wanted to learn the ropes of a working ranch, men like he'd been, hungry to work their way up. He also had four groomers and two trainers as well as the cook for the ranch hands, a robust woman named Hazel.

The noisy rumble of voices quieted as he entered and stepped up in front of the crowd. "As you know, my daughter, Lucy, is still missing. At this point, we don't have any leads. Carter Flagstone, the man we originally believed responsible, did not abduct her. Last night Kim received a ransom call and we made a drop, but the kidnappers escaped with the money and there's still no word on Lucy."

A few sympathetic whispers resounded through the room. Brandon searched each of the men's faces, looking for anyone suspicious, overly nervous or anxious to leave.

"The sheriff has questioned whether or not someone close to me might be involved," Brandon said. "I don't want to point fingers or put anyone on the spot, but if any of you have seen or heard anything or have any information that might help me find Lucy, I'm doubling the reward."

He studied the faces again as he finished his speech, hoping they understood that he meant business.

If one of them had betrayed him, he'd regret it.

KIM BATTLED PANIC as she raced into Brandon's study. Earlier, she'd seen him store extra cash in a safe behind his desk so she dropped to her knees to open it. Dammit, what was the combination?

She tried his birthday, then his wedding date—she'd emblazoned that date in her head years ago—but neither worked. Frustrated, she banged her fist on the safe. She could call Johnny, but he'd demand to go with her just as Brandon had, and this time she refused to take any chances.

She had to open the safe. She racked her brain, then punched Johnny's birthday, the day Brandon had graduated from school, the day Carter was arrested. Then she tried Brandon's sister's birthday, but none worked. Sweating, she checked her watch.

It would take her a half hour or more to reach the address the kidnapper had given her. She had to hurry.

On a whim, she plugged in her own birthday and was shocked when the safe door clicked open. The realization gave her pause, but she didn't have time to dwell on the reason Brandon had used it. She grabbed the cash inside and counted it. It wasn't nearly a hundred thousand, but if she padded the bottom of the bag, maybe it would appear to be. And she didn't have time to call Johnny or wait on Brandon for more.

She grabbed the bag Johnny had used to bring his money to them and stuffed the money inside. Thankfully Brandon had walked to the dining hall, so she grabbed his keys and rushed outside to his truck.

Her heart raced as she climbed in, turned on the ignition and the headlights, and sped down the drive.

"I'm coming to get you, Lucy," she whispered. "Just hang on, sweetheart. This time I'm bringing you home."

She felt for the gun in her purse. If the kidnapper didn't bring her daughter to her, she'd shoot him and make him tell her where Lucy was. Nothing was going to stop her this time.

She'd find her daughter or she'd die trying.

THE MEMORY OF LUCY riding Spots sent a wave of despair through Brandon as he walked past the stable. But his cell phone trilled, and he quickly connected the call. "Woodstock."

"I ran that background check on your employees' financials like you asked," Hollister said. "A name popped up, Farley Wills. Apparently he was heavily in debt, but he recently deposited a hundred thousand to a new account."

Brandon tensed. Farley was in his sixties with a gimp leg and a wife who hadn't been able to work in years. Where had he gotten that kind of money?

"It's not the whole million you gave up in ransom, but it's suspicious."

"He's here on the ranch. I'll find him," Brandon said in a clipped tone. "Anything on that corporation?"

"It was a dummy corporation. I'm trying to trace the person behind it. Whoever set it up knew what they were doing and intentionally covered his tracks."

Brandon silently cursed, then hung up and jogged back to the house to pick up his SUV. When Brandon had hired Wills, the older man had been out of work for months, his wife ailing, and he'd sold off the house he'd owned for forty years to pay off his wife's medical bills. He also had a son in Afghanistan.

Suspicions nagged at Brandon. He'd felt sorry for the old man and had wanted to help him.

He rounded the corner and froze. The SUV was gone.

Kim.

His heart started hammering like a jackhammer. Had she heard from the kidnapper? If so, why hadn't she called him?

Fear clawed at his chest, and he rushed inside. "Kim!"

A quick look in the kitchen, and there was no note. Nothing to tell him where she'd gone.

Dammit.

She'd been upset. Had she simply taken a drive?

Or had she gone to meet the kidnapper?

He'd hoped that last night made a difference, that she trusted him, that she wouldn't do something foolish. But if she'd gone to meet the kidnapper alone, she might get herself killed.

God…he couldn't go on if he lost Kim and Lucy….

Hand shaking, he punched in her cell phone number, but it rang once, twice, three times, four, five, then rolled over to voice mail.

"Kim, where are you? Call me. I have to know you're all right."

Their earlier conversation echoed in his head, and he realized she blamed him for losing Lucy, for insisting he accompany her on the drop.

Hoping she'd turn to Johnny, he punched his friend's number and sighed in relief when Johnny answered.

"Johnny, have you heard from Kim?"

"No, why? What's wrong?"

"Kim and I had an argument. I went to question my employees, and when I got back to the house she was gone."

"Gone?" Johnny asked. "What do you mean *gone?*"

"I mean she's not here." Brandon paced the kitchen, tunneling his hand through his hair. "She took my SUV and left without a note. I tried her cell, but her voice mail picked up. I was hoping she'd come to you—"

"Dammit, Brandon, I haven't heard a word. What did you two argue about?"

"Us. Lucy. She blames me, man." Emotions thickened Brandon's throat.

Johnny muttered a curse. "She's just upset, Brandon—"

"I know that, but she's right. I'm Lucy's father, I should have kept this from happening."

"Stop it," Johnny said in a sharp tone. "Blaming yourself won't bring Lucy back. We have to figure out where Kim is."

Brandon paced the floor. "She must have heard from the kidnapper, and she's gone on her own—"

"And may be walking into a trap," Johnny said in a strained voice.

Yes, and it was his damn fault.

"Did Hollister turn up anything?"

Brandon bowed his head into his hands, pinching the bridge of his nose to stem his emotions. "He's checking out that dummy corporation." He snapped his head up. "And he found some discrepancies in one of my ranch hands' financials. I'm going to see him now."

"I'll drive out there."

"No," Brandon said. "I may need you for backup later. Wait until I call."

Johnny made a frustrated sound. He didn't like it but he agreed, and Brandon located the keys to the old pickup he kept in one of the storage barns and jogged outside. It took him three attempts to start the damn thing, but finally the engine chugged to life, and he sped toward the cabin where Wills lived. He tried to remember if he'd seen the old man in the dining hall, and recalled seeing him limping toward the back door.

Night was falling, the sun dipping behind the tops of the oaks, casting gloomy shadows as more storm clouds brewed. As he parked, he spotted Farley loading something in the back of a truck.

Luggage? Was he about to take off?

He screeched to a stop and jumped out, braced to tear the old man apart.

"Where are you going, Wills?"

Farley turned to him, wiping sweat from his forehead with a worn handkerchief.

"Nowhere," he said. "Just going to haul off some trash."

"You were at the dining hall," Brandon said. "You know what I'm up against."

Guilt lined the man's weary face. "Yeah, I was there."

Farley dropped his head and stared at his crooked

fingers. His hands were shaking and when he raised his head, fear and resignation settled in his eyes.

"I'm sorry, Mr. Woodstock. You're a good man." He rubbed his hand over his mouth. "I...didn't mean to hurt anyone. Especially that little girl."

Brandon's blood went cold. He had to swallow twice to make his voice work. "What are you saying? You didn't mean to hurt her?" He grabbed Farley's arm and forced him to face him. "What did you do to my daughter?"

Wills's eyes went wide. "I...I didn't do anything to her, I swear."

"Then what the hell did you mean?" Brandon said through clenched teeth. "And where did you get that hundred thousand?"

Wills's face crumpled. "My son, he was killed in a bombing in Afghanistan," he said in a raw voice. "He had a life insurance policy."

Brandon's chest clenched. He'd had no idea. But that didn't explain his comment about Lucy.

"I'm sorry, Farley. Honest, I am. I didn't know."

Farley shrugged. "Imagine that. My son died a hero when I'm half-crippled and still here. And now I'm using that money to try and save my wife."

Sympathy for the man ballooned inside Brandon. But he still had questions. "That's awful, Wills," Brandon said. "But please tell me. What did you mean about hurting Lucy?"

Wills rubbed at his gimp leg. "I don't know if it has anything to do with her disappearance or not. Maybe I'm wrong."

Brandon gripped his arm. "Listen, just spit it out and let me decide."

"I hate to get anyone in trouble—"

"Tell me, dammit!"

Wills wheezed another labored breath. "Boyd Tombs," Wills said. "The night Kim and Lucy came here, I saw him out near the northern pasture. He was with someone, they were talking in low voices."

"What were they talking about?"

"About you. About Lucy."

"What about her?"

"That she was your little girl."

The air tightened in Brandon's lungs. "Who was he talking to?"

The man's brows crinkled. "Your wife, Mr. Woodstock. That's why I didn't say anything. I…thought Boyd and her were sneaking around, you know, having an affair. It never occurred to me they'd do something like kidnap your child." He tugged his arm away from Brandon, his frown deepening the lines around his eyes. "I mean, why would they?"

Brandon had no idea.

It wasn't like Marty needed money. And he thought she'd moved on. That she was getting remarried.

Then again, his ex-wife had an obsessive streak and was spoiled rotten. She always got what she wanted, and he'd realized after marrying her that she'd set her hooks into him.

Her pride was hurt when he'd asked for a divorce, but he'd never considered the fact that she'd do something to get revenge on him.

"Did you hear anything else?" Brandon asked. "Maybe they mentioned a trip they planned to take, some place they were going?"

Wills shook his head. "No, but Boyd hasn't been back to work the last two days. Called in sick, so it started me thinking."

Brandon nodded. "You should have come to me sooner, Farley."

"I know," Wills said. "But I ain't been myself since Roy died. And it's not like I heard them say they were going to do something or seen 'em take Lucy."

His voice cracked and the tears in his eyes made Brandon realize the man was suffering.

But so was he. And his little girl was, too.

And how the hell had Marty found out that Lucy was his?

"Did they say anything else about Lucy? Or maybe mention a place they might meet up?"

Wills shook his head. "No. Like I said, that's all I know."

Brandon raced toward his truck, punching the sheriff's number as he sped back to the house.

"You think your ex-wife kidnapped your daughter?" Sheriff McRae asked after Brandon explained his conversation with Wills.

"I don't know," Brandon said. "But if Marty told Tombs Lucy was my child, he could have orchestrated it. Then again, it's possible they planned it together. Can you send some cops over to her house and her father's ranch?"

"I'm on it," the sheriff said. "And what about this Boyd Tombs?"

"See what you can find out on him." He parked the truck and flew into the house, then ran to the computer to check Tomb's background information. Maybe there was an address....

But as he sat down in front of the computer, the opened email caught his eye, and he frowned.

Marty had sent him a message. She still loved him? She wanted to help?

Was she delusional?

Dammit, he had to get to the bottom of this.

He scrolled through the employee data, then cursed as he spotted one of Boyd's references. Tyler Anglin, the foreman for Marty's father's ranch.

Boyd must have met Marty while at her father's estate. She'd probably seduced him into doing whatever she wanted.

So it was possible they had conspired to kidnap Lucy.

But who had been behind it? Boyd or Marty?

Boyd probably needed the money. But he'd met the young man and couldn't imagine him concocting such a scheme.

Marty was the smart one. Manipulative. Cunning. Charming.

The one who had a motive to hurt him.

His mind raced as the last months of their marriage played through his head. The fights over everything. His ranch. Traveling. Her desire, no, *obsession,* to have a baby.

His refusal because he feared he'd pass on that genetic disease.

If Marty had wanted revenge and discovered Lucy was his child, she could have easily manipulated Boyd into helping her.

But if Marty was behind this, surely she wouldn't hurt Lucy....

Still, they had found that blood. And he didn't know Boyd well enough to be certain that if he lost his temper or things turned sour between him and Marty, that he wouldn't,

He groaned, his heart heavy. He had to think like Marty.

If she had Lucy, she wouldn't hide her at her father's or at her own place.

So where would she take her?

KIM SLOWED THE SUV, the headlights blazing ahead to reveal a small log cabin nestled in the midst of acres of woods. Flower beds bloomed in reds, yellows and golds, and a welcoming wreath hung from the front door.

This cabin looked homey, like a vacation retreat, not deserted and run-down like Baxter's property.

What was going on? Did she have the address correct?

She glanced down at the notes she'd scribbled, then rechecked the road sign and the number on the box and frowned. Yes, this was it.

Still, the hairs on her nape stood on end. The kidnapper had sent her here for a reason.

To trap her into some false sense of safety?

Because Lucy was here?

Or to kill her this time?

Inhaling to calm her nerves, she cut the engine, removed the gun from her purse, tucked it in the back of her jeans and pulled her shirt down to cover it, then grabbed the duffel bag. Leaves and twigs snapped and crunched beneath her feet as she climbed out and looked around.

The caller had insisted she put the money in the wood box on the porch. But she didn't intend to leave without her daughter this time, so she stayed alert as she walked up the stone walkway to the porch. The cabin sat on a hill overlooking the river which raged over jagged rocks below. The drop-off was steep, and she shivered, wondering how deep the water was at that point, and trying to fight the panicky feeling that the kidnapper might have killed Lucy and dumped her in the river.

A twig snapped from the direction of the woods. Insects buzzed. Leaves rustled. Shadows moved from the thicket of trees nearby. Then the hiss of a snake.

Another sound from the left startled her, and she jerked around, but a figure moved toward her and knocked her to the ground.

She kicked and fought, but something hard and sharp slammed against her temple. Stars swam in front of her eyes. Then the world spun in a drunken rush and she fell into the darkness.

Chapter Sixteen

Brandon searched his memory banks for Marty's friends' names.

The only two he could think of were Andrea Meriweather and Susie Peterman. Both were just as spoiled and materialistic as Marty. Both drenched in diamonds and designer outfits and servants—the lifestyle Marty had wanted.

The one he abhorred.

Hell though, he didn't know their numbers. But he would find them. He tried the phone book, but as he'd feared, their numbers were unlisted. What now?

Remembering that both of them belonged to the garden club in town, he looked that up on Google and found the number. But the snooty woman who answered refused to cooperate.

"We are not in the habit of releasing our members' personal contact information."

"But this is an emergency," Brandon shouted.

The phone clicked silent.

He cursed and punched in the P.I.'s number. "I need two phone numbers." He explained his reasons and gave him the women's names and within minutes the man had hacked into the information.

"Thanks," Brandon said. "And find out anything you can on a man named Boyd Tombs. He worked for my ex-wife's father before coming to work for me. I think he may be involved in the kidnapping."

"I'm on it," Hollister said.

Brandon hung up and punched in Andrea's number. A servant answered, "Meriweather residence."

He identified himself as Marty's husband. "I need to speak to Andrea. This is an emergency."

"I'm sorry, Mr. Woodstock, but Miss Meriweather is out of the country. She flew to Paris yesterday for a fitting for her bridal gown. I believe your wife went with her."

Brandon slammed down the phone, his hands shaking. Was he wrong about Marty?

Maybe. But Marty could have faked the trip.

Hopefully, Susie had some answers.

He punched in her number and waited and waited, but the phone rolled over to voice mail. Dammit.

He heaved a breath, then listened to the recording. She was out of the country, as well.

Sweat streamed down his face as he paced to the porch and stared out. He had to think. Where would Marty take Lucy? Someplace secluded…

Not to Baxter's deserted overgrown property. No, that had been a setup. Marty could have easily bought that land under a dummy corporation's name, then planned with Boyd to kill Kim and leave her there so no one would find her.

The thought sent a wave of terror through him, and he groaned.

Clenching the porch rail with a white-knuckled grip, he inhaled another deep breath. He didn't have time to give in to his emotions. He had to think. Get into Marty's head and figure out what she would do.

She was spoiled, rich, liked nice surroundings. But if she had kidnapped Lucy, that meant she was desperate. Hell, she might have walked off the ledge from obsessive to crazy.

Think like Marty, think like Marty....

If Marty had Lucy, she'd want to be comfortable because Marty herself was not the camping/low-rent type. She preferred the niceties in life.

But she wouldn't take her someplace where a witness would see her with Lucy.

No, she'd find a remote location to hide.

He closed his eyes, his head aching from wracking his brain. Then it hit him.

If she'd kidnapped Lucy to get revenge on him, she'd take her to a place that had meaning for both of them.

His mind ticked back to the trips they'd taken, most of them arranged by her or her father. All fancy hotels with servants.

But a hotel would be too risky.

Another memory surfaced. For their honeymoon, he'd found a secluded cabin perched on the San Antonio River. It had been far enough from the downtown area and tourists to be secluded, but the cabin itself was plush and cozy and…miles from civilization.

Brandon had met the owner on a business trip he'd made for Marty's father, and Marty had surprised him by loving the place. She'd insisted they return there for a romantic getaway last year, wanted them to conceive their child at the special place where they celebrated their wedding night.

But he had not been in the mood for romance or making a baby.

Because he hadn't loved her.

He'd still been in love with Kim, and now he wondered if she'd sensed that all along. If that was the reason she'd abducted Lucy and led Kim into this trap.

If so, then they were both in terrible danger.

His heart racing, he snatched his keys again, jammed his cell phone in his pocket, checked his weapon and jogged outside to the truck.

He had to get to Marty before she took Kim and Lucy away from him forever.

A BRIGHT HAZE OF LIGHT blinded Kim as she slowly regained consciousness.

"Dammit, she's still alive," a man's deep voice mumbled.

"Get rid of her." This voice from a woman. "I'm going to take care of the kid."

A shudder rippled through Kim as she felt herself being dragged through the dirt. Her head was throbbing, her vision blurry as the light faded and the darkness tried to swallow her again. But she fought it, summoned every ounce of strength and determination she possessed and began to fight.

She had to find Lucy.

She kicked at her attacker, swinging at him wildly. One fist connected with his chest, and he grunted, then slammed the butt of the gun against her temple. She cried out, the sting of blood trickling down her forehead into her eye.

But she refused to give up.

Grappling for a stick or rock, anything to use as a weapon, she clawed the ground but came up with a handful of dirt instead. She threw it at him, and he cursed, then slapped her across the face so hard her vision blurred. Then he dragged her deeper into the woods. The sound of the river crashing over rocks drifted toward her, and panic seized her. Was he going to throw her into the river?

Another blow to the head, and she passed out again. When she stirred sometime later and tried to move, her hands and feet were bound and her head throbbed. She screamed and fought to undo the bindings, but the bright light blinded her again. A flashlight. Someone was shining it straight into her eyes.

"Who are you?" Kim cried. "Why are you doing this?"

A bitter laugh echoed, a feminine one that sounded shrill as it caught in the wind.

"You had to come back after him, didn't you?" the woman snarled.

Kim tasted dirt as he shoved her into some kind of hole. A grave.

Dear God, they were going to kill her and bury her out here and no one would ever find her.

Battling full-fledged terror, she squinted through the blinding light and saw the silhouette of a man and woman standing above her.

"Where's my little girl?" Kim cried. "What have you done with her?"

"Lucy's fine," the woman snarled. "But she won't be your little girl anymore. She's going to be mine."

"No!" She clawed at the dirt, trying to climb from the grave, but the woman kicked her in the face. "Lucy is my daughter," Kim screamed as she spit blood and dirt. "Let me have her."

"You'll never see her again," the woman screeched. "And you'll never have Brandon. He's *my* husband, and he and I will have the family I should have had all along."

The truth dawned on Kim in mind-numbing shock. "Marty?"

"Yes," Marty said bitterly. "You tried to steal him away from me by getting pregnant. But it didn't work five years ago and it won't work now. Brandon and I were meant to be together."

Kim choked on tears. "When he finds out what you've done, that you terrified his daughter, he'll hate you."

"You don't understand," Marty shouted. "He'll never know I had anything to do with the kidnapping. Lucy never saw me, only my partner."

Another chilling laugh and Kim realized Marty was unstable.

"That's right," the man said. "Marty and I will get away scot-free with all your money."

But Marty suddenly wheeled around and aimed her gun at the man. "Sorry, Boyd. I appreciate your help, but it's over."

"Marty, honey, what are you doing?" the man asked in a shocked tone.

"This was never about the money," Marty said.

The click of the trigger punctuated the night. The sound of the bullet being dislodged followed.

Kim braced herself for the impact, but realized that Marty had shot her accomplice. She screamed as he collapsed on the ground, and his hand dangled over the edge, fingers outstretched toward her.

God help her, she had to escape.

"What are you doing?" Kim cried. "Marty, this is insane. You—"

"You're the crazy one for thinking you could steal Brandon back."

"Marty, please—"

"Now you're going to die, and then I'm going to be the hero."

Kim struggled to see if the man was alive, but he lay sprawled on the ground, unmoving. "Hero? But you killed him and kidnapped Lucy—"

"Like I said, Brandon will never know the details," Marty shouted. "Once you're dead, I'll call him and tell him I discovered one of my ranch hands kidnapped Lucy, that I tracked him down and found her."

"He'll never believe you," Kim cried.

"Of course he will. I found the kidnapper burying you, so I had to shoot him to protect myself. And there will be no one to dispute my story."

"He'll know," Kim cried. "He—"

"No, he won't. Boyd's prints are all over the shovel, all over the ropes he tied you up with. I'll tell them I found you in the grave he dug for you and tried to revive you, but you were already dead." She laughed again, a hollow, empty sound that resounded with her victory. "He'll be upset at first, and Lucy will, too. I'm sure. But don't worry, Kim, I'll comfort them both. And soon, soon they'll forget all about you, and I'll be Lucy's new mommy and Brandon and I will live happily ever after."

Kim shook her head in despair, struggling to free her hands so she could fight, but it did no good.

Marty aimed the gun at her and fired.

The bullet pierced her chest and burned a hole in her heart. Lucy and Brandon's faces danced before her mind, then tears rolled down her face, and the world slipped away.

BRANDON EASED UP the drive to the cabin, senses alert for trouble. But suddenly a car raced toward him, flying down the dirt road, pebbles and debris spewing from the back.

The headlights nearly blinded him, and he swerved to dodge the vehicle. Then the car swung sideways and screeched to a stop. His tires chewed gravel, and he nearly slammed into a tree, but managed to stop inches from it. Adrenaline flooding him, he swung the door open and felt for his gun, scrutinizing the situation.

The car was a black Mercedes.

Marty's.

She threw the door open, her eyes wide with shock as she ran to him. "Brandon, dear God, I was coming to get you. I was going to call you as soon as we escaped."

Brandon stilled, his pulse racing. "We?"

"I found Lucy," she said, her breath rasping in short pants.

"What? Where is she?"

Marty grabbed his hand and hauled him toward the car. When he peered through the glass, he saw his little girl huddled in the back clutching a rag doll, her eyes wide with terror.

When she saw him, she broke into a squeal and shoved at the door. He jerked it open, unfastened her seat belt and dragged her into his arms. Emotions overcame him, and he buried his face against her sweet, soft hair and rocked her back and forth, his chest heaving with sobs. For a moment, all he could do was hold her, silently thanking God she was alive.

Her little arms clenched his neck so tightly he could hardly breathe, but he didn't care. He never wanted to let her go.

"I wants Mommy," Lucy cried.

Her soft cry brought him back to reality, and he swallowed more tears and pulled back long enough to look at her.

"Lucy, honey, oh, God, I'm so glad to see you." He searched her face for the truth. "Are you okay? Are you hurt? What did they do to you?"

Her face crumpled. "I was scared, Daddy. I wants Mommy!"

His gaze flew to Marty. "Where's Kim?"

Marty gave him a sympathetic look. "I'm sorry, Brandon. Kim's back there in the woods. I tried to save her, but it was too late." Her words came out clipped, short, breathlessly as if she'd been running from someone.

"I have to go to her," Brandon said.

Marty caught his arm. "No, I told you it's too late. Boyd Tombs, a man who used to work for Daddy, he shot her." She reached for him, but he pushed her away, pressing Lucy's head into his shoulder and holding her tight.

"Don't lie to me, Marty. I—"

"It's true," Marty said in a shrill voice. "Boyd used my computer to set up this dummy corporation to buy some land. He was desperate for money, and knew I still loved you so he targeted you. When I arrived, Kim was here, and they were struggling." She released a noisy breath and folded her arms around her middle with a shiver. "He'd already dug a grave for her body, and he shot her and shoved her in it."

"No!" Lucy wailed. "I wants Mommy…"

An icy chill enveloped him. Was he too late to save Kim?

He staggered backward and managed to remain

standing as he dissected Marty with his eyes. She could be lying. Biding time while Boyd buried Kim and she fed him this bogus story.

"Shh," he whispered, trying to soothe Lucy. "Marty, where is Kim?"

"I told you, she's in the woods," Marty said. "I tried to rescue her, but Boyd pulled his gun on me, and I had to shoot him to keep him from killing Lucy." She reached out a hand, her eyes begging him to believe her. "I couldn't let him hurt her, because I love you."

Brandon's chest constricted. She sounded so sincere that he didn't know what to believe.

But he didn't intend to leave without Kim.

He'd built The Woodstock Wagoneer for her. She was the only woman he'd ever loved.

And he hadn't even told her.

Chapter Seventeen

Brandon tried to calm Lucy by rubbing her back. "Take me to Kim, Marty."

Marty shook her head. "It's too late, Brandon." She placed a hand on Lucy's shoulder as if to soothe her, but Lucy's fingers dug into his neck as she tightened her grip.

Panic warred with rational thought as he studied his ex-wife. If she had saved Lucy, then he owed her. But if she had orchestrated the kidnapping and killed Kim, she had to pay.

He had to know the truth. Play along. If she was the kidnapper, she was cunning and maybe delusional.

"I don't care. I have to see her." He intentionally lowered his voice. "If you really tried to save her, then you'll do as I ask. Then we can call the police and you can explain what happened."

Her eyes flickered with uncertainty, but she slowly nodded in concession, and the smile she gave him didn't quite meet her eyes. "All right. I wanted to spare you, but if you insist."

Hell, yes, he insisted.

He gestured toward his truck. "Get in. I'll drive."

"Daddy?" Lucy shivered as he settled her in the backseat. "I'm scared. I wants Mommy."

"I know, sugar," he said, indecision and guilt weighing on him. If Kim was dead, it might traumatize Lucy even more to see her in the woods. But what if Marty was lying?

What if Kim was hurt and needed help?

He kissed Lucy's cheek. "Hang in there a little longer, Lucy. I'm going to find Mommy."

He just prayed to God that she was still alive.

Tension drilled at his neck as he climbed in and started the engine. He glanced over his shoulder and Lucy pulled her knees up to her chest, wrapped her arms around them and buried her head against her arms.

Marty squeezed his arm. "I'm so sorry, Brandon. I really am. I know you've always been loyal to your friends."

And he had been loyal to her when they were married even though every time he'd crawled in bed with her, he'd closed his eyes and imagined making love to Kim instead.

Had she known it?

His headlights beamed across the dark path as he wound through the wooded drive. Memories of his honeymoon taunted him.

Then their anniversary in an attempt to rekindle the romance and make a baby.

That night he'd known he couldn't pretend to love her anymore. It wasn't fair to either one of them to live a lie, so he announced that he wanted a divorce.

He cut his eyes toward her, but she gave him a sly smile, part sympathy, part coy female, and his instincts roared.

Had she lured Kim here to kill her because this was the place he'd asked for a divorce?

The woods shrouded the moonlight and stars, cloaking it in a gloomy dismal gray as he parked at the cabin. Once this place had looked homey and inviting, but now it looked eerie.

"Why didn't you call 911 or the sheriff when you figured out Boyd had Lucy?" Brandon asked as he opened the door and pushed himself out. "Hell, why didn't you call me?"

"I didn't know for sure," Marty said. "So I followed Boyd here. Then I saw him kill Kim, and I shot him. But I was afraid Boyd might not be dead, that he might kill me, too." Marty stepped out, her face strained in the moonlight. "All I could think about was rescuing Lucy."

"Daddy!" Lucy cried.

He opened her door, leaned over and hugged her. "Stay here, sugar. I'm going to find Mommy and see if she's hurt."

"I don't like that wady," Lucy whispered in his ear.

Her childish intuition made his spine tingle with apprehension.

"I'll be back in a minute," he said, then kissed her cheek.

He had to move fast. If Kim was alive, every second counted.

He grabbed a flashlight, then sucked in a breath and headed toward the woods. Marty followed, her low throaty sounds of sympathy grating on his nerves. The wind whistled, shaking trees, and a mountain lion howled somewhere close by. The sound of vultures screeching above made him pick up his pace.

Brandon waved the flashlight across the ground, aiming it toward the woods. "Where are they?"

"Over there." Marty caught his arm, her voice soft. "I'm so sorry, Brandon."

He shook off her touch and jogged toward the thicket of trees, then the clearing by the river. But as he grew nearer, his pulse thumped in a sickening rhythm.

Boyd was lying on the ground, blood soaking his shirt and chest, his limp hand dangling over the edge of a hole. A grave.

Just as Marty had said, Kim lay inside, bloody and still, her face a stark, milky white.

Blood soaked her chest....

A deep shout of protest clogged his throat, and he started to kneel to check on her, but Lucy's scream ripped through the air, and he spun around. Dear God, she'd followed him and was staring at her mother in shock.

Marty shifted next to Lucy and put a hand on Lucy's shoulder to soothe her, and Brandon snapped from his own fog of shock and jumped inside the grave beside Kim. His hands shook as he touched her cheek with his thumb; then he leaned over to see if she was still breathing. With the wind wailing and Lucy's cries, he couldn't tell, so he lifted her wrist and checked for a pulse.

He closed his eyes, praying for a beat, then waited, his heart slamming in his chest. Two seconds passed. Five. Ten. Twenty.

A half a minute.

Dear God, please...

Finally he felt a small thump. Slow and shallow but she had a pulse.

Relief surged through him and he hugged her to

him. "Kim, baby, you're alive. Hang in there, I'll call an ambulance."

Slowly he eased her back down, then ripped off the end of his shirt, folded it and pressed it to her chest, applying pressure to stop the bleeding. Then he reached in his pocket for his phone. But the click of a gun made him jerk his head up.

"No, you don't," Marty said in a steely tone.

Her eyes looked wild and crazed as she pointed the gun at Lucy's head.

"Daddy!" Lucy cried. "Help, Daddy!"

His body stilled, and for a moment, he thought he'd die from the sheer terror of seeing Marty with that gun trained on Lucy. Then a cold numbness washed over him. He had to save Lucy and Kim, no matter what.

Even if it meant lying and indulging Marty's fantasies.

KIM DRIFTED IN AND OUT of consciousness, the air around her smothering, the acrid scent of death pulling at her.

She was weak. Drained. Her mind spinning in and out of dark places. Then intermitent, sweet images of Lucy and Brandon coaxed her back.

Brandon's voice whispered to her, urging her not to leave them. She'd felt his hands on her chest, her wrist, felt his arms around her, holding her, warming her, chasing away the chill of death.

And then Lucy...she was alive.

But she was crying.

Kim struggled to make her voice work, to call out to her daughter and reassure her that she would never let anyone hurt her again. That she wouldn't leave Lucy without a mother.

Then Marty's icy, sinister tone broke through the haze. Marty who'd shot her...

Kim wiggled her finger, clawing to get up and save herself. She had to fight to keep from disappearing into the darkness.

Marty was crazy. She wouldn't let her win.

But suddenly she felt Brandon leaving her. She coughed, trying to call his name.

"Please, hold on, Kim. I have to save our daughter."

His low voice penetrated her pain-addled brain, and she nodded. Or at least she hoped she did. But her limbs grew numb. She felt weightless as if she was leaving her body, drifting up into the sea of emptiness. She didn't want him to go. Didn't want to lose him again.

But she was dying. Holding on by a thin thread of light...watching the scene from somewhere above her body...

Her life didn't matter if Lucy was in danger. Brandon had to save their daughter.

Then she was alone. Brandon was gone, and the voices grew distant.

But his words drifted to her through the haze of pain.

"I'm here, Marty," Brandon said. "Just put the gun down and let's talk."

"Brandon," Marty said softly. "You know all I wanted was a family with you."

"We can have that now," Brandon said. "Kim is not going to make it. I can see that. But you and I...we can have what we wanted all along."

"Daddy!" Lucy cried.

"Shh, baby, trust Daddy. Everything will be fine."

His words drove a knife through Kim's heart. Had

she imagined him holding her before? That kiss in her hair? Him telling her to hold on?

She felt herself floating again, at the same time sinking lower and lower into the well of darkness. Then she heard death calling her name....

Brandon was right. She wasn't going to make it.

Tears burned her eyes as the weight on her chest grew heavier, and her breathing slowed.

Dear God...Brandon and Marty were going to raise Lucy together....

And she wouldn't get to see her little girl grow up.

BRANDON FORCED A CALMING SMILE for his daughter, but Lucy's little body shook with terror. Dammit, he wanted to pull her into his arms and protect her more than he wanted to live.

But Marty was obviously deranged, and he had to play along with her delusions until he could wrestle the gun away from her.

"Marty, sweetheart, listen to me. Please put down the gun."

Angry desperation flared in her eyes. "You said vows to me, Brandon, not her." She waved the gun toward the grave where Kim lay bleeding and barely breathing. Lucy tried to pulled away, but Marty's grip on her tightened.

"Let me go," Lucy cried.

"Not until your father admits that he loves me," Marty said. "That we can all be a family together."

They had never been a family. Their marriage had been more of a business arrangement than a romance, but he kept a leash on his tongue.

His lungs fought for a breath as he reached out his hand and slowly moved toward her. "You're right,

Marty," Brandon said. "I did say vows and so did you. Now if you love me, you'll put down the gun. You don't want to frighten my daughter."

"*Our* daughter," Marty spat out. "We can raise her together, Brandon." She ran a hand over Lucy's curls, but Lucy cringed and leaned as far away from Marty as she could. "I always wanted a little girl, but you wouldn't let me have one. And Boyd broke into Kim's to get her, but you stopped that, too."

"I know, and I'm sorry," Brandon said in a low, soothing voice. "You know I was just afraid because of Joanie. But it was wrong of me to deny you."

"Yes, it was," Marty said, her hand wavering. "We could have had it all just like I planned."

"Marty—"

"But no, Kim messed it up by going to that ranch," Marty said in a seething tone. "I knew if you ever saw her in person, you'd realize Lucy was yours and you'd leave me."

Brandon froze, ugly suspicions rearing themselves in his head. "You knew Lucy was mine? How?"

Marty pulled Lucy in front of her, stroking her shoulders as if she was trying to prove that she could be a good mother.

"I saw Kim going into the doctor's office one day. I figured she'd try to seduce you back after you proposed to me, so I snuck into her medical files. And there it was. She got knocked up to trap you."

That wasn't true. If Kim had wanted to trap him, she would have told him about the baby, but she hadn't.

"It doesn't matter," Brandon said. "All that matters now is that we keep our little girl safe. So put down the gun, Marty, then we can talk."

"All I wanted was for us to have another chance,

Brandon." She glanced at Lucy. "I can be a good mommy, Lucy. I gave you my doll Mags so you wouldn't be scared. I used to sleep with her when I was little."

Lucy's lip quivered as she threw the rag doll into the dirt. "I don't wants your old doll. I want Lambie and Mommy and Spots."

Lucy's tirade triggered Marty into a rage. "You ungrateful little twit! Boyd would have hurt you if I'd let him."

"You're a meanie," Lucy cried. "You hurted my mommy, and she's the bestest mommy in the world...." Lucy gulped back a sob. "Just ask Daddy."

Brandon inched closer, trying to telepathically tell Lucy to trust him. Then Marty looked up at him with tears in her eyes, and whirled the gun toward him. "I don't want to hear about your precious Kim. She was always there, in our bed, in our house, in...your heart."

"Marty, wait—"

"You never loved me, did you?" Marty said sharply. "You used me to get what you wanted, then you ran back to her and your bastard child!"

He didn't give a damn what she said about him, but she would not bad-mouth his little girl. Giving Lucy a slow nod, he rushed Marty. Lucy stomped on Marty's foot at the same time, and he knocked Marty's arm upward. A gunshot fired into the air; Lucy screamed, then dove into the grave beside Kim.

"Stay down, Lucy," he shouted as he and Marty fought for the gun.

Marty kicked at him and clawed at his eyes with one hand, but he swung his hand up and chopped at her wrist. She buckled in pain and released the weapon. It sailed through the air and landed at the edge of the embankment.

Marty was like a wild dog, biting and kicking and screaming. She managed to wrench free and dove for the gun. He lunged for it at the same time, but she snatched it and swung it up toward him. He ducked sideways to avoid a bullet, then threw himself on her and knocked her to the ground. Using his body weight, he tried to pin her down and wrestle the gun from her hand, but she grabbed a rock and slammed it against his temple. The blow momentarily disoriented him and he fell sideways.

She took advantage of the moment and crawled away. She was heaving for a breath. "You bastard, you lied. You always lie!"

He pushed to his hands and feet, saw her backing near the edge of the drop-off to the river. Lucy's cries echoed over the raging water.

"Stop it, Marty," Brandon said. "You aren't well. Let me get you help."

"I don't need any help," Marty screamed, once again waving the gun. "I just want what's mine, and you're mine!"

She aimed the gun at Lucy again, and fury surged inside him. He charged forward with a bellow. "I'm not yours. I never was."

He hit her so hard, she stumbled back and lost the gun. Rocks and pebbles skittered downward as her foot slipped on the edge. Marty screamed and threw her hands out, grappling for something to hold on to.

Brandon reached for her, but her arms pummeled wildly, and she careened over the edge into the river below. Her scream boomeranged through the air, hollow and chilling.

He raced to the edge and looked down into the water.

One second he thought he saw her body, the next she disappeared into the raging current.

Chapter Eighteen

"Daddy!"

Lucy's cry tore Brandon away from the river edge, and he ran to his daughter. She was hunched over Kim, her face filled with terror.

"Mommy won't move, Daddy," Lucy wailed.

Brandon stepped down into the grave, lifted Kim, then carried her over to a giant oak and lowered her to the grass. Lucy scrambled behind him, then slumped down and pulled Kim's hand between her tiny ones.

He held his own breath as he checked Kim's pulse.

Low and thready, but still beating.

Thank God.

"Stay with her, honey," Brandon said. "Keep telling Mommy you love her while I call an ambulance."

Lucy nodded and swiped at the tears tracking her cheeks, then pressed Kim's hand to her chest. "Pwease wake up, Mommy. Daddy and I loves you. You gots to wake up now."

Brandon's heart broke. Poor Lucy had suffered so much these last few days. She could not lose her mother.

He quickly punched 911. "I need an ambulance and the sheriff. A woman has been shot." He gave the dispatch officer the address, then called Johnny to fill him in.

Johnny cursed. "Marty escaped?"

"I doubt she survived," Brandon said. "She was never a very strong swimmer."

"I don't give a damn," Johnny said. "How's Lucy?"

"Okay physically. But she's scared to death that Kim won't make it." Brandon's voice cracked. "So am I."

"Hang in there with her," Johnny said. "She's tougher than you think, and she has a lot to live for. I'll meet you at the hospital."

Brandon ended the call and prayed Johnny was right as he went to sit with Kim and Lucy. Kim looked so pale, her face ashen in the moonlight, her hands cold and clammy. Her breath was so shallow he could barely discern it, and she'd lost a lot of blood.

Lucy looked up at him with such trust that he pulled her into his lap and hugged her, then together they whispered loving words to Kim while they waited on the ambulance.

An hour later, Kim was in surgery when Johnny rushed in with Rachel and her six-year-old son Kenny.

Lucy ran to him and Johnny swung her up in his arms and squeezed her hard. "Hey, pumpkin. You okay?"

She nodded, but tears blurred her eyes. "But that doctor made me go with him. I don't wike doctors."

Johnny and Brandon exchanged a silent look of understanding, then smiled gently at Lucy. "Doctors help us get better, Lucy," Johnny said gently.

She nuzzled her head against his chest. "I know, but I don't wike 'em."

"Tombs held her at the cabin, so she had a TV and

toys," Brandon said, lowering his voice. "At least Marty kept her safe." Until the end when she'd become so deranged she'd tried to kill him and Lucy.

But he didn't want to remind Lucy of that terrifying moment. Not that she was likely to forget it. The psychologist who had interviewed Lucy said to expect nightmares, that Lucy might need counseling.

Rachel edged up next to Johnny while Kenny watched, wide-eyed and curious. "How's Kim?"

Brandon clenched his fists. "I don't know yet. She's in surgery."

Sheriff McRae suddenly appeared, his face a mask of granite as he strode toward them. "Woodstock?"

Brandon and Johnny both pivoted, and Rachel reached for Lucy. "Come on, sweetheart, why don't I take you and Kenny down to the vending machine to pick up some snacks."

Lucy glanced at Brandon, and he gave her a brave smile. "Go on, sugar. I'll be right here."

Rachel hugged Lucy and took Kenny's hand, and they disappeared down the hall.

Sheriff McRae cleared his throat. Brandon had briefed him when he'd arrived at the cabin, but the ambulance had already arrived, and he'd left the sheriff to investigate while he accompanied Kim.

"We processed the crime scene," Sheriff McRae said. "Fingerprints on Marty's gun match ones we found in the house as well. And preliminary forensics confirms that it was the same gun that killed Boyd Tombs."

"What about that blood at the cabin?"

"It was Tombs's. Apparently your daughter bit his arm and he lost some blood."

Brandon gave a small smile. "Good for Lucy."

"So what was Marty's story again?"

Brandon sighed and scrubbed a hand over his chin. "She claimed that Boyd shot Kim and that she tried to save her, that she shot Boyd in self-defense."

"There was a shotgun inside with Tombs's prints on it, but we didn't find a gun on Tombs at the gravesite," the sheriff said.

"So she was lying as I suspected," Brandon said. "Marty was behind the whole scheme. She suspected Lucy was mine years ago, and snuck into medical records to confirm it."

Surprise registered on Johnny's face. "But as long as you stayed with Marty, she didn't tell you or didn't do anything."

Brandon nodded. "When I asked for a divorce, she was afraid I'd go back to Kim. And then when we both wound up at the Bucking Bronc Lodge—"

"She knew you'd figure out the truth," Johnny finished. "And the ransom request was just a ruse to make it look like a kidnapping for money."

Brandon turned to the sheriff. "Did you find her body?"

"No." The sheriff tugged at his belt. "We searched all along the riverbank, but nothing. No footprints or signs she'd climbed out of the water. We called in some dogs, so I'll let you know."

"What about the ransom money?" Johnny asked.

"We recovered all of it. Your ex had hidden it at the cabin."

A mixture of sadness and anger filled Brandon. He had never loved Marty, but he had cared about her. He still couldn't believe she had become so unhinged.

"I'll let you know if we find her body," the sheriff said.

"Have you contacted Marty's father?" Brandon asked.

The sheriff frowned. "Yeah. He's not taking it too well. He claims Tombs must have planned the kidnapping, and believes Marty was the hero."

Brandon's eyes narrowed. "She held a gun to my daughter's head," he said. "She was obsessive, and… crazy. She thought we'd just leave Kim there, and she and I would raise Lucy together. She was no hero."

"She obviously needed psychiatric help," Johnny muttered.

The sheriff nodded. "Well, it looks like it's too late now."

He just hoped it wasn't too late for Kim.

Voices nearby made Brandon look up, and a female doctor approached. "Are you Kim Long's family?"

Brandon and Johnny both waved her over.

"I'm Dr. Mervon," she said, then shook each of their hands. "Miss Long made it through surgery all right. Although the bullet came within inches of her heart, it missed the major arteries." Dr. Mervon paused. "The next twenty-four hours will tell. After that, she's going to need lots of rest and TLC."

Brandon heaved a sigh, and Johnny practically swayed with relief.

"She'll have that," Brandon said.

Johnny nodded. "Count on it."

The next two hours dragged by while they waited on Kim to come out of recovery. When she was finally moved to a room, they were able to see her.

"Take Lucy first," Johnny said. "She needs to know that her mom is going to survive."

Brandon nodded and lifted Lucy in his arms. "Come on, sugar. Let's go see your mommy." He stroked

Lucy's hair from her forehead. "Just remember Mommy was hurt so she'll be sleeping, and she has tubes in her, but those tubes are giving her medicine and air to make her feel better. So don't be scared, all right?"

Lucy lifted her chin in a brave gesture, and his heart swelled. Still she clung to him as he carried her inside. Kim looked starkly pale beneath the hospital lights, the tubes and monitors beeping.

"Mommy?" Lucy whispered.

He eased Lucy down beside Kim on the bed, warning her to be careful not to pull out Kim's IV.

Lucy curled up next to Kim and laid a hand on her mother's cheek. "I loves you, Mommy. Hurry up and gets better so we can go home with Daddy and ride Spots and have more picnics."

The doctor had stressed that they couldn't stay long, so he told Lucy to kiss her mother good-night, then carried her back to Rachel and Kenny. He grabbed a cup of coffee while Johnny visited Kim.

When Johnny emerged, he looked worried, but marginally better. "If you want to take Lucy home, I'll stay here."

"No way." Brandon gestured to his little girl, who was yawning as she cuddled next to Rachel. "Why don't you drive them back to the ranch for the night? I want to be with Kim." His voice broke. "I have to."

Johnny stared at him for a long moment, then offered his hand. "Thank you for saving her and Lucy, Brandon."

Emotions flooded Brandon, and he shook Johnny's hand, although he couldn't speak for the fear and guilt needling him.

This whole mess was his fault. Lucy being kidnapped. Kim being shot. Even Marty, who'd been hurt because he couldn't love her.

Kim had to survive so they could be the family they should have been five years ago.

He just hoped when she woke up that she could forgive him.

VOICES FLOATED IN AND OUT of Kim's consciousness as she struggled to open her eyes. Her body ached, her limbs felt weak, and terrifying images of Lucy being held by Brandon's wife bombarded her.

Where were they now? Had Brandon and Marty gone away with Lucy?

No...Brandon had been here. And so had Lucy. She'd heard their voices.

Or had she been dreaming?

She faded again, disappearing into a thick veil of darkness. She was being swallowed by it, consumed by the pain. She couldn't move. Couldn't breathe.

Then something heavy settled over her mouth and face, shutting out the light.

Another voice. Shrill. Sinister. Chilling.

"You're going to die, Kim. Then Brandon will love me."

Marty? She was here? In the darkness?

No...it was the drugs. She was in the hospital.

Hard fingers closed around her neck. Kim felt a dampness on her face and then something soft like a pillow. Then it was smothering....

She tried to open her eyes, but when she did, all she saw was a sea of black.

Terrified, she tried to scream, but something was cutting at her windpipe.

No...she had to fight. But her arms and legs and her voice wouldn't cooperate.

"You should have died back there at the cabin," the voice rasped against her ear. "But you will now. If I can't have Brandon, neither will you."

Oh, God...Marty. She *was* here and she was trying to kill her.

The pressure over her face and mouth became more intense, cutting off her oxygen. She gagged, gasping for a breath.

God help her... She was going to die. And she'd never see Brandon or Lucy again.

Chapter Nineteen

"Brandon," Johnny said, hesitating. "Are you sure you don't want me to stay?"

Brandon's heart thumped at the uncertainty in Johnny's eyes. Years ago, he, Carter and Kim had been best of friends. None of them would have questioned the other.

But things had changed. They'd grown up. Made mistakes.

"I know I hurt Kim, Johnny, and if you don't trust me, I understand." His voice warbled as he tried to control the anguish rolling through him. "But I love your sister with all my heart, and I want us to be a family." He shifted awkwardly. "I just hope she can forgive me for...this mess."

A slow smile titled Johnny's face. "You two were meant to be together." He punched Brandon's arm like they used to do when they were kids.

"You didn't think so when we first got together," Brandon said wearily.

Johnny gave him a sheepish look. "Hey, I was just being a big brother. I had to know it would stick so you wouldn't hurt her."

"But I did," Brandon said, sobering. "I swear to you, Johnny, I'll make it up to her."

Johnny pulled him into a man-hug. "Don't tell me, buddy. Tell my sister."

Brandon smiled, then gave a nod. "I'm going to do that right now."

Johnny released him and went to gather Rachel and the kids and take them home. Brandon walked down the hallway, for the first time in ages feeling hopeful that he might have the life he'd dreamed about when he was eighteen.

But when he opened the door to Kim's room, he saw a shadow hovering above Kim, a dark shadow. Then he saw Kim's feet moving as if she was struggling and realized she was fighting off an attacker.

Marty! Dammit, she'd survived.

He lunged forward, grabbed her around the neck and yanked her away from Kim.

"Let go of me, she has to die!" Marty screamed.

Brandon knocked the pillow off of Kim's face and saw her heaving for oxygen as he contained Marty in a stranglehold. "Stop fighting, Marty," he growled. "It's over."

Kim shoved at the bedding, the machines by her bed beeping loudly. A second later, a nurse and doctor raced in.

"Take care of Kim and call security!" Brandon shouted. "This woman tried to kill her."

Marty seemed to finally realize that she'd lost, and she slumped in his arms and broke into hysterical sobs. He still didn't trust her though, so he maintained his grip around her, determined to make sure she didn't escape this time.

The nurse gave him a sympathetic look but hurried to Kim, reattaching her oxygen while the doctor checked her vitals. "She's going to be okay," she said.

"Get her out of here!" the doctor ordered, gesturing toward Marty whose wails grew louder.

Marty kicked and screamed as he dragged her through the door and down the hall to the waiting room. He was grateful when security rushed up and took over.

KIM SLUMPED AGAINST THE BED, exhausted and drained, and so weak from the gunshot and surgery that she had no energy.

But she would live. She had fought Marty off, and she would survive. Still, despair rooted itself inside her. Brandon had saved her life.

But it had cost him dearly. She had heard him tell Marty they would be a family, and he had built the ranch and the house Kim had dreamed of for the two of them.

Brandon might have made love to her out of desperation or pity because they'd both been afraid for Lucy.

But Marty was the one he'd chosen as his wife. And even if he asked her and Lucy to stay with him, she could never be with a man who didn't love her.

BRANDON DIDN'T KNOW whether to hate Marty or pity her. Her clothes were muddy and damp from the river, her hair a wild nest, scrapes and scratches marring her arms and legs where she'd fought to escape the river.

As soon as the sheriff appeared and took her into custody, he rushed back to Kim.

The nurse was checking her vitals as he entered.

"Is she all right?" he asked.

The nurse nodded. "She just needs rest."

He wanted to pull her in his arms and confess his love, but she looked exhausted and in pain, and she closed her eyes as the medication took effect.

So he claimed the chair by her bed and waited through the night. Each time she moaned or labored for a breath, he thought of Marty and the guilt settled deep in his bones. He had made a mess out of all their lives.

Would he be able to fix them now?

THE NEXT FEW DAYS dragged by for Kim. Between the painkillers knocking her out, her exhaustion, and the ordeal of giving her statement to the police, she felt drained.

Johnny and Rachel had brought Lucy to visit her, and Brandon had barely left her side. Which confused her even more.

He had apologized for Marty's actions, and she sensed he blamed himself. But she also sensed he was grieving for his lost marriage, and she didn't know how to respond to that.

A few times, she thought he was going to say more, but she hadn't wanted to hear a confession about him loving Marty so she had cut him off.

Now she was being released, she couldn't postpone the conversation they needed to have any longer. She would make it short and to the point. She'd have to, or she'd break down and pour out her heart.

The nurse knocked, then pushed a wheelchair in, and Brandon appeared behind her, his jaw set and strained.

"Ready to go home?" the nurse asked with a cheerful smile.

Kim gritted her teeth as she moved her legs to the side of the bed.

"Actually I'm going to my brother's ranch to recu-perate."

Brandon's eyes flared with surprise. "What?"

"I think it would be best," Kim said, then lowered herself into the wheelchair.

"No, we're going to my place," Brandon said in a voice that brooked no argument. "Rachel and Johnny and the kids are there waiting."

Kim clamped her lips closed. She didn't intend to argue in front of the nurse. "Fine. Then Johnny can take me and Lucy to the BBL afterwards."

Brandon glared at her, and she shivered, knowing he would fight for Lucy, and Lucy would want to stay....

Tension stretched between them as he helped her in his SUV and they drove toward his ranch.

"What's going on, Kim?" Brandon finally asked. "Why do you want to go to Johnny's?"

"I just need to rest, Brandon. And Lucy is comfort-able there."

"She seems happy at my ranch."

"That was before she was kidnapped," Kim mur-mured. "If you remember, we only came there because we were in danger."

Brandon tensed. "You're taking Lucy away because you blame me, don't you?"

Kim started to speak, but he threw up his hand to silence her. "I understand, Kim. It was my fault. All of it. I screwed things up badly with you, and Lucy...she was caught in the middle." His voice broke. "For that, I'll never forgive myself. But Lucy is my daughter and I'm not giving her up now."

Kim sighed wearily and leaned her head on her hand. "I know you love Lucy," Kim began. "But you were married to Marty and you're grieving for her now. For your marriage."

"You have no idea how I feel about Marty."

Kim shut down. "I don't want to talk about this now, Brandon." She closed her eyes on a heavy sigh. "I can't. I'm too tired."

And on the verge of tears.

Brandon muttered an oath, then fell into silence as he drove them the rest of the way home.

As soon as he parked at the ranch, Lucy, Johnny, Rachel and Kenny bounded out. They had strung banners on the porch welcoming her home, ones she was sure Lucy had helped make.

"We're having a party for you, Mommy," Lucy said as she launched herself into her mother's arms. "We gots cupcakes and ice cream, and Daddy made you a surprise."

Kim glanced at Brandon, confused, but Lucy was so excited, she couldn't disappoint her so she smiled and played along as they swept her inside for a homecoming celebration.

And as she watched Johnny with Rachel and her son and Lucy with Brandon, her heart ached even more. She wanted this place to be a home for her and Brandon and their daughter.

But she couldn't forget that he had built it for the woman he had married.

Not for her.

Brandon watched Kim kiss Lucy good-night before he carried Lucy up to bed. He couldn't let Kim leave the ranch. If she did, he might lose her forever. The memories of finding her in that grave and Marty trying to smother her still haunted him day and night.

Still, she had erected a wall between them during the welcome-home party. A wall he had to break down.

By the time he descended the stairs, Kim was walking toward the steps as if to retire to her room.

Now that he'd had her in his bed, he wanted here there again. Forever.

"We need to talk."

"I'm tired, Brandon, I—"

"I know you need rest. But you can't keep running away from me."

Kim averted her eyes. "I'm not."

He tilted her chin up with his thumb. "Yes, you are. And God knows you have reasons. I hurt you years ago, and if it hadn't been for me, for Marty, you and Lucy would never have been in danger."

"It's over now, Brandon," Kim said, meeting his gaze. "But I can't stay here, not in this house, not when you built it for her. I can't be a replacement for the woman you love."

Brandon stared at her, stunned.

How could he have been so dense?

He tugged her hand and urged her to sit down. "Listen to me, Kim, you have it all wrong. I never loved Marty."

Her soft gasp echoed between them. "But...you left me to marry her...you said—"

"I know what I said, but it was a lie." The events that had led to that decision haunted him. "Back then, Joanie was so ill. I...promised her I'd find a way to bring her home, to get her out of that terrible nursing facility. I thought they were abusing her there."

Kim gasped. "Oh, my god, I didn't know."

"I know," Brandon said. "I didn't have proof, but it

was a feeling. That's the reason I married Marty. Her father offered me a job, a future, money, a way to take care of my sister." He'd never regretted anything more in his life. "And I took it. Then Joanie died, and I'd lost you, and Johnny hated me. I wanted to leave Marty then, to tell you the truth, but I figured you'd never let me back into your life, and then you'd—"

"Slept with Carter," Kim said in a raw voice.

"And I couldn't get that image out of my head—"

"Just like I couldn't get the image of you making love to Marty out of mine."

He nodded, sighing heavily. "So I tried to make it work with Marty and built my ranch."

Kim worried her bottom lip with her teeth. "And you were happy?"

"No," he said. "How could I be when I was still in love with you? When it was *always* you?"

Shock flickered across her face, then pain and regret, and he brushed her cheek with the pad of his thumb.

"The thing is, Kim, I think Marty always knew that. She sensed that I wanted you, not her. And even if I had wanted her, our goals were too different. She wanted to travel, live in society. I wanted this place, the land, to work with my hands."

Kim gestured around the rustic den. "But you built this house for her."

Brandon shook his head, feeling foolish and hopeful at the same time. Foolish because on a whim, he'd built Kim's dream home when he'd had no idea if she'd ever forgive him.

And hopeful that she still loved him.

He gathered her hands in his. "No, Kim, I built this house for you."

She narrowed her eyes in confusion. "Because you found out about Lucy?"

He shook his head again. "I didn't know about Lucy until we met at the Bucking Bronc," Brandon said. "Until that night you were attacked. When I saw her... those eyes, that's when I knew."

"But I heard you tell Marty that the three of you would be a family."

His chest clenched. "God, Kim, she had a gun on Lucy. I was just playing along with her to get the gun away. I would have said anything at that moment to save you and Lucy."

Tears glittered on Kim's eyelashes, and he lifted her hands and kissed them. "Come here, I have to show you something."

She frowned, but stood and he led her to his bedroom and opened the door. Kim's mouth gaped when she stepped inside.

"It's...different. You changed it?"

He nodded. "This week while you were in the hospital, I've been busy." He dropped her hands long enough to walk over and open a wooden hope chest. Then he removed the magazine he'd saved from years ago.

"Brandon..." Emotions tinged her voice. "That's the magazine—"

"The one you liked." He flipped it open, revealing dog-eared pages. "When I built the house, I showed the architect and decorator these photographs. I tried to replicate the things you wanted."

"The porch swing," Kim said in awe. "The bed upstairs, the colors..."

She raked her hand over the new pale-green-and-white quilt he had bought this week. He'd painted the room a soft sage green and had Rachel help him find decorative pillows and touches similar to the one in Kim's dream room.

"Marty never lived here, Kim. She's never even been in this house." He cupped her face between his hands. "I built this house hoping to bring you here and win you back someday." He gestured toward the new bedding. "And I changed the room this week because I wanted to give you the room of your dreams. To let you know that this is not my ranch, not my house. Not my home. It's *ours*."

"Oh, Brandon…" Tears of joy filled Kim's eyes.

"I love you, Kim," Brandon said. Then he dropped to one knee and removed a velvet ring box from the hope chest and held it out for her. "You're the only woman I've ever loved. I know I made mistakes, but I promise that I will love you and Lucy, that I'll protect you and cherish you the rest of my life. We can live here and grow our family, and we can both help out at the Bucking Bronc Lodge." He paused, then opened the box to reveal an antique set diamond. "Will you marry me, Kim?"

Kim's heart gushed with love, and she reached for Brandon and threw her arms around him. "Yes. I love you, too, Brandon. I always have."

He kissed her fervently, then slid the ring on her finger, and Kim's heart swelled with love and happiness as he picked her up and deposited her on the bed.

At eight, she'd followed a rough-and-tumble, troubled teenaged cowboy around, enamored with everything he said and did.

At eighteen, she'd fallen hopelessly in love with him.
At nineteen, she had given birth to their child.
And now, finally, he was going to be her husband.

* * * * *

SUSPENSE

Heartstopping stories of intrigue and mystery—
where true love always triumphs.

Harlequin

INTRIGUE

COMING NEXT MONTH
AVAILABLE MARCH 13, 2012

#1335 CORRALLED
*Whitehorse, Montana:
Chisholm Cattle Company*
B.J. Daniels

#1336 COWBOY TO THE MAX
Bucking Bronc Lodge
Rita Herron

#1337 SECRET IDENTITY
Cooper Security
Paula Graves

#1338 LAWMAN LOVER
Outlaws
Lisa Childs

#1339 A WANTED MAN
Thriller
Alana Matthews

#1340 FINDING HER SON
Robin Perini

You can find more information on upcoming Harlequin® titles,
free excerpts and more at www.HarlequinInsideRomance.com.

HICNM0212

New York Times *and* USA TODAY *bestselling author*
Maya Banks presents book three in her miniseries
PREGNANCY & PASSION.

TEMPTED BY HER INNOCENT KISS

Available March 2012 from Harlequin Desire!

There came a time in a man's life when he knew he was well and truly caught. Devon Carter stared down at the diamond ring nestled in velvet and acknowledged that this was one such time. He snapped the lid closed and shoved the box into the breast pocket of his suit.

He had two choices. He could marry Ashley Copeland and fulfill his goal of merging his company with Copeland Hotels, thus creating the largest, most exclusive line of resorts in the world, or he could refuse and lose it all.

Put in that light, there wasn't much he could do except pop the question.

The doorman to his Manhattan high-rise apartment hurried to open the door as Devon strode toward the street. He took a deep breath before ducking into his car, and the driver pulled into traffic.

Tonight was the night. All of his careful wooing, the countless dinners, kisses that started brief and casual and became more breathless—all a lead-up to tonight. Tonight his seduction of Ashley Copeland would be complete, and then he'd ask her to marry him.

He shook his head as the absurdity of the situation hit him for the hundredth time. Personally, he thought William Copeland was crazy for forcing his daughter down Devon's throat.

Ashley was a sweet enough girl, but Devon had no desire

HDEXP0312

to marry anyone.

William had other plans. He'd told Devon that Ashley had no head for the family business. She was too softhearted, too naive. So he'd made Ashley part of the deal. The catch? Ashley wasn't to know of it. Which meant Devon was stuck playing stupid games.

Ashley was supposed to think this was a grand love match. She was a starry-eyed woman who preferred her animal-rescue foundation over board meetings, charts and financials for Copeland Hotels.

If she ever found out the truth, she wouldn't take it well.

And hell, he couldn't blame her.

But no matter the reason for his proposal, before the night was over, she'd have no doubts that she belonged to him.

What will happen when Devon marries Ashley?
Find out in Maya Banks's passionate new novel
TEMPTED BY HER INNOCENT KISS
Available March 2012 from Harlequin Desire!

HDEXP0312

Harlequin® Desire

ALWAYS POWERFUL, PASSIONATE AND PROVOCATIVE.

**NEW YORK TIMES AND USA TODAY
BESTSELLING AUTHOR**

MAYA BANKS

**MIXES BUSINESS WITH PLEASURE
WITH ANOTHER INSTALLMENT OF**

PREGNANCY
PASSION

The last feather in businessman Devon Carter's
cap would be to enter a business partnership with
Copeland Enterprises. But to achieve this he must
marry Ashley Carter—the boss's daughter. Ashley is
everything Devon didn't think he wanted—but she's
about to change his mind.

TEMPTED BY HER
INNOCENT KISS

Available wherever books are sold this March.

*Celebrate the 30th anniversary of Harlequin® Desire with
a bonus story from reader-favorite authors. A different story
can be found in each book this March!*

HD031273156